The Greening of Thurmond Leaner

The Greening of Thurmond Leaner

A NOVEL

MICHAEL ZAGST

DONALD I. FINE, INC.
New York

Library of Congress Catalogue Card Number: 85-81871
ISBN: 0-917657-65-9
Manufactured in the United States of America
10 9 8 7 6 5 4 3 2 1

This book is printed on acid free paper. The paper in this book meets the guidelines for permanence and durability of the Committee on Production Guidelines for Book Longevity of the Council on Library Resources.

For Ed Zagst and Anna Zagst,
two of the angels.

1

LEANER TURNED ON THE
air conditioner in the motel room before carrying in
his suitcase and golf clubs. He had driven too far in
one stretch, and all the decent rooms in town had filled
up. He drove off the interstate and found himself in a
section of the town that resembled one big junkyard.
The cheap motel he had managed to ferret out amid
the rusted automobile frames and debris actually did
accept scrap metal in lieu of cash for their rooms. His
own room still held the heat of the day within it. He
let it cool off while he went out on the streets again
to search for a telephone.

At the pay phone he got hold of the operator.

"I'd like to make a collect call to area code 713, and
that number is 488-0499."

"And what is your name?"

"Thurmond Leaner."

While the number was ringing, the operator began
to speak.

"You could have dialed that number yourself, Mr.

Leaner, and a local operator could have handled the charges. This way, I have to do the dialing."

"Thank you for telling me," Leaner said.

"Hello?"

Leaner smiled as he imagined her carrying the phone from the hall to the bedroom.

"A collect call to anyone from Thurmond Leaner."

"I'll accept."

"Go ahead, Mr. Leaner. And remember what I said about dialing."

"Thurmond, where are you?"

"I'm in the Volunteer State," he said. "Tennessee."

"I've thought a lot about you today, honey. I keep thinking you're going to walk in the front door any minute. I miss you."

"I wish we were together too," Leaner said, "but we're not, so I guess there's no use in going on about how I could be there or you could be here when it isn't that way."

"When will you get to your sister's house?"

"I hope by tomorrow evening. That'll give me a full week to rest up before the tournament. I hope to hit a few buckets of balls on her land. Amelia said it was okay with her. I hope it still is."

"Why do you keep saying 'I hope,' Thurmond? Is something wrong?"

"No, no. I'm just tired," Leaner told her. "Since leaving Houston the only people I've talked to are gas station attendants, desk clerks and waitresses. I covered the length of Arkansas in one sitting. My rear is numb. Do you know what they call Arkansas? The Land of Opportunity. I saw it on the license plates there. It's a pretty place, Arkansas. The room I got tonight isn't air conditioned yet. I'm keeping my fingers crossed that it cools down some. What's new at home?"

"What? You're jumping all over the place.... What's new at home? Well, that kid you chased off the dirt pile hasn't been back. I haven't seen him anywhere in the neighborhood. What did you say to him?"

"Which time?"

"When he was throwing dirt clods on the car."

"I just said I wasn't that wild about washing the car, and would he please cut it out."

"And he stopped then?"

"No, he kept it up. I went back outside and asked him why he wasn't home jerking off like normal kids his age. So I imagine he's in his room choking his chicken."

"I wish you hadn't left," she said.

"We discussed this," Leaner said. "We agreed. I'm playing in the tournament, then I'm coming home."

"Yes, but why the Catskills? Nightclub comics get their start there. Not golfers."

"Lauren, I don't care how well you're playing, you just can't jump in with the big guys. They'll tear you to pieces. The competition won't be as stiff where I'm going. Anyway, the ball is already rolling. It would be silly to turn back now. What are you doing tomorrow?"

"What am I doing tomorrow? Is that what you asked me right in the middle of something else? Oh, I get it. You've changed the subject. You're good at that. Let's see, I must be doing something. Oh, yeah, I'm buying the dog a new flea collar."

"I'll call you from Amelia's," Leaner said.

"Right," Lauren answered. "Drive carefully, honey."

* * *

Leaner had taken a big step to leave home when he did. Until now, he hadn't made a dime from golf, other than dollar-a-hole side bets with friends of his. It was when none of his friends would take him on anymore that he looked into the possibility of turning pro; his game had shown steady improvement from the day he had first touched a club. Now Leaner couldn't drop in on a driving range without closing the place down. Other patrons dropped their own clubs on the ground, practically encircling him as he stepped out of his car. They would buy the buckets of balls for him just to watch him at work, picking up a stray tip when they could. By then Leaner had the ability to call his shots. He would aim for the fifty-yard marker with a wedge, then the hundred with a nine iron, and so forth. At three hundred yards the range was fenced, and Leaner could bounce about a fifth of his drives off the barrier. The driving range was his proving ground. And when he developed the touch to move the ball left and right, incorporating controlled hooks and slices into his game, that was the time, he decided, to become serious about golf as a career. It had taken years of obscurity and work to get to this point.

Slowly his game approached consistent par, sometimes dipped into the high sixties. But months passed for every stroke he shaved. Although his game evolved at a frustrating pace, he loved getting out and slamming the ball around. The fact that he excelled at it was a bonus. Still, only if he could break par consistently would he rest easy. And he wasn't there yet. Which was why he would choose to drive 1,500 miles for his debut as a pro.

In the meantime he had to make a living. One summer, home from the University of Texas and the friendly climate of Austin, he hired on as a nail driver with a roofing company. He could feel his biceps developing, as well as his forearms. Near the end of August the roofing company backed out of a small room addition, and Leaner somehow convinced the customer that working alone he could save them money and construct a better room than they had imagined. It was the end of September when Leaner realized that school had started without him that semester, and he was self-employed in the home improvement business.

Construction work turned out to be the perfect complement to golf. Both required analytical, abstract calculations, whether it was how the slope of a green toyed with gravity to take a golf ball for a ride, or how in the world to support a fifteen-foot gazebo using only wood and concrete. Books on both subjects helped, but the *doing* was the ticket.

He wasn't thrilled to be in school anyway. It was a great place to meet girls, but Leaner changed majors as frequently as other students changed the oil in their cars. He didn't want to be an anthropologist. He was a golfer and a builder. For a long time it had been a tossup between the two.

When Leaner returned to the motel, the woman who had checked him in was sweeping a pile of dirt out to the street. She reminded him of somebody, and he had trouble placing her for a moment. Then it dawned on him that she was the image of Potty Suggs, a tar-eating boy who had lived in Leaner's neighborhood when they were both growing up. One day Potty had told Leaner between chews of tar that his family was moving to

Tennessee, where his father had found a job as a prison guard. So in a way the resemblance made sense. But he couldn't bring himself to ask the woman whether she was related to someone who, years ago, pulled tar out of the cracks in the street and ate it like taffy.

In his dismal little room he took a shower, and as he dripped on the floor he put a damp hand in front of the air conditioner, hoping the machine would blast a chill into the room at any moment. Meanwhile he had dried off and stretched out on the bed to study his road atlas. Rather than checking the mileage state by state, he opened the atlas to the national map, aligning a shoelace along the highways he intended to use. While measuring the shoelace against the scale to see how far he had to go the next day, a drop of water fell from his brow, landing somewhere near Pittsburgh. He stood up to check the thermostat and motor speed of the air conditioner, but it was already cranked up to maximum output. It never did cool off, but he was so tired from driving that he dropped off to sleep anyway.

For Leaner, the United States was composed of four roughly defined regions: out west, down south, up north and back east. In spite of these categories he felt that living in Houston lent him no directional sense of place, other than an occasional down and out. Living in the city was like that for him. But clear-cut boundaries fascinated him. Crossing state lines was always a thrill, though that was small potatoes compared to passing from Central to Eastern time. He had pulled over now to the side of the road, wanting to linger a few minutes. He studied shadows and watched birds as they flew from one time zone to the other. He wished he had a camera to make a record of the place, expecting at any moment to be overwhelmed by a pleasant, back-east mood, a soaring sensation of nostalgia and expectation. But then a motorist stopped to see whether he was having car trouble, forcing him to go back on the road. Actually his complaints to Lauren about the scarcity of human contact had been little more than idle conversation; Leaner was more of a loner than he wanted to be. His sister and even Lauren had called him introverted, and he guessed he was.

In the afternoon Leaner pulled off the interstate for something to eat. There was a snack bar adjacent to a rest area, and the parking lot was nearing capacity. He was somewhere in West Virginia. He walked the length of the counter inside, looking for an open seat. The crowd inside had a locker-room weariness, an edge brought on by hours and hours of driving. They were all just passing through. He found the restroom and washed his face, splashing in the sink like a sparrow. He stood up straight and searched for paper towels, passing stalls and dripping on the cement. For a moment he considered using toilet paper, then he noticed a hand dryer. He pushed the button on it and a rush of warm air blasted out of the chrome fixture. He rubbed his hands together, then when he saw no one watching he crouched beneath the blower. It was like peering up a chimney, but he got his face dried off. When he was finished he saw a small boy halfway through the door staring at him.

"Hey, Dad!" the boy yelled. "Come look at what this man is doing!"

Leaner squeezed past the boy and stood behind someone at a water fountain. A disappointed voice from inside the restroom echoed out, "Too late, Dad. You missed him." When the man was through drinking, he stepped to one side. Leaner took a long gulp.

"That water's good and cold," the man said, and Leaner nodded his head.

"Dad! Come look at the commodes they have here."

Leaner finished his drink and took a couple of steps backward.

"I swear, I don't know how some people can raise more than two kids," the man told him. "Don't get me wrong. They're fine kids. Both of them. But eighteen hundred miles in a station wagon can give anyone the willies. You know what I mean? Even a restroom is an adventure."

Leaner wiped his mouth. "That water *is* good," he said. He wanted to escape.

He wasn't feeling that hungry anymore and decided to settle for a canned drink for the road. Just as he was about to drop some coins in the machine's slot, the bathroom boy shot in front of him, pulled out a screwdriver and started jimmying the coin slot for loose change. Leaner didn't see the boy's father now, so he tapped on the little shoulder in front of him.

"Hey, sonny," Leaner said, "you know you shouldn't do that. You're old enough to know better."

"Piss off," the boy said. "Or else I'll get my Dad."

Leaner checked the dining area. No one was watching him. Even if they were, they looked too exhausted to do anything. Leaner pinched the flesh above the boy's collarbone just as the father stepped up.

"What's going on here?" the man asked. "Tommy, what are you into now? Let's go, son. Get in the car."

Leaner rocked back on his heels, hands in his pockets. "Just a minute," he told the man. "You ought to know something. It's just a minor irritation, but you might consider catching it early if you can."

"What are you getting at?"

"That boy of yours. He belongs in a strait jacket or a military school."

Leaner watched the man for a reaction. He didn't know what he might have started. There could be a brawl in a matter of moments, a regular saloon fight that could spread to the parking lot like wildfire. He was a little relieved that the man said nothing. The guy's neck swelled up and reddened, but he backed down and led his boy outside.

Leaner was glad he had said it. He had a tendency to hold things back, but was beginning to overcome it. He took his drink outside and sat on the top of a picnic table, and became aware of some movement in the underbrush a few yards away. A bit alarmed, he kicked a crust of bread near his feet into the leaves. Almost immediately a pair of rodents poked their heads out of the leaves. Were they small rats, or large mice? There was something admirable in their efficiency, and Leaner looked around for another scrap to give them, then suddenly realized how much his attention was being diverted from the job at hand—another tendency of his. He finished the drink and climbed back in the car.

It was quite late when Leaner reached Pennsylvania's Allegheny Forest. It was a little disorienting to be surrounded by huge trees on a mountain road at that time of night. He knew that his sister's property bordered somewhere on the forest, but that wasn't much help at the moment. How big was the Allegheny, and which side of it was Amelia on?

He searched the glove compartment for the map Amelia had sketched for him, and pulled over on the shoulder of the road to have a look at it. He tried projecting the scrawls and scratches on the piece of paper into the three-dimensional mess he found himself in. Beelines and hunches were out of the question because he didn't know where he was.

"All right," he said out loud. "To get there, I've got to start from Cyclone. But where the hell is Cyclone?"

Leaner was afraid the town would be so small that he could pass through it if he so much as sneezed. If that were true he could have already missed it among the hills and winding country roads. He turned the car around, deciding to wake up someone in a building he had passed a few miles back. He didn't much like dealing with a stranger that way but what choice did he have?

Just as the building came into view Leaner noticed a road sign. Apparently the building and two or three other structures were the township of Cyclone. Leaner wanted to honk his horn and announce to the residents of the hinterlands that he was an independent professional golfer with a keen sense of direction.

Outside the town Leaner found the iron ore road from Amelia's map, put his headlights on bright and pressed his face almost against the windshield. On a ridge, a gravel drive sloped to one side, and he stopped the car in order to read the mailbox. He had found it. As his car rolled down the driveway he could see a flickering light about a quarter-mile away. He came closer, and a houserobed figure appeared in the light, standing on the porch a moment, then gliding like a ghost to his car as he parked.

"Very, very good," Amelia said as he opened the car door. She bent forward and kissed his cheek. "It's hard enough finding us in the daytime. I'm impressed."

"I got a little turned around in the forest." Leaner smiled.

"That nasty old forest. A man up the road saw a bear here night before last. About four hundred yards from here."

"Oh, my God," Leaner said, and smiled again. "You know I have a problem with strangers."

She laughed. "You must be exhausted. Come on in."

Inside the house Amelia explained that the children were doubling up for the duration of his visit, so he could have a room to himself. "But stay as long as you like. Move right in if it suits you."

Leaner hadn't realized how tired he had become until his knees nearly buckled on him in the living room. He had never experienced a feeling quite like it. He gripped the arms of a chair, wondering if somewhere someone was possessed by constant knee buckles, living in a house with railings along every wall.

"Why don't I leave my things in the car tonight? No use in clanking around at two in the morning."

"Try three," his sister corrected him. "Upstairs to the left is yours. Sleep as late as you like. I'm going back to bed before I really wake up." Amelia went halfway up the stairs and paused. "My little brother from Texas is here. God."

"Good-night," Leaner told her.

2

HE SLEPT SOUNDLY. WHEN
daylight awakened him it seemed only minutes had
passed since he had crashed into the pillow. He looked
to the foot of the bed and saw that someone had brought
in his suitcase. Not hearing anyone moving about, he
took some clean clothes to the bathroom and began
grooming himself for the day. He descended the stairs,
the only household noise a hum from the refrigerator.
He looked through a couple of kitchen cabinets and
found some instant coffee. Tilting against a counter
while the water came to a boil, Leaner tried to yawn.
He knew there was one in him but was having a time
getting it out. With his mouth wide open he filled the
coffee cup and moved to the outside porch, contorting
and stretching his face until he loosened a toehold on
the yawn.

"You should eat some breakfast."

Leaner was so startled that he spilled some coffee.
He turned in the porch chair to see how Amelia had
appeared so quietly.

"How many eggs do you want?"

"I don't want any," Leaner said. "Thanks, anyway."
Even the sight of food this early made his stomach
queasy. He needed some time-killing to bring him to
his senses. "Amelia, please don't sneak around like
that. You really put a scare in me."

"That's from too much city living," she said. "Learn
to relax, Thurmond. It only took me about fifteen years
to calm down." She stood behind Leaner's chair and
started massaging his neck and shoulders.

"That feels good," he said.

"I know. That's why I'm doing it. Little brother, I'm
so glad you came up here. It's been too, too long."

"You could have flown to Houston any time."

"Thurmond. Look. Look out there. Would you leave
this unless you absolutely had to?"

Leaner gazed across a clearing near the house.
Amelia's backrub was so soothing he felt nearly hyp-
notized. He wasn't sure whether what he was looking
at was a natural meadow, or a portion of the forest that
had been cleared for the house. Beyond the meadow,
the trees were so thick they blocked the sun. In the
distance somewhere he could hear a stream.

"It sure is nice here," Leaner said. "How many acres
are yours?"

Amelia patted her brother on the back to indicate
the end of the massage and took a chair at his side.
"Three or four hundred. It's hard to say because so
much of it is uphill. As far as the eye can see, at any
rate. I didn't pay for it all at once, just so I wouldn't
get lazy and not work. It was like, 'I'd better get to
work so I can pay off the farm.' Charles and Jean are
crazy about the place too. They're out taking a hike

right now. You don't know how excited they are that
you're here. When they got up this morning the first
thing they asked was what time you came in, and if
you brought them any lizards."

"That's the damnedest thing," Leaner said. "I remembered how they went after the lizards the last time
y'all came to Texas. Whenever I go outside this time
of year I see them by the dozen. Packs of them. Really.
Then, when I got ready to leave, I spent a couple of
hours looking for some. I didn't see a one."

"That's too bad," she said.

"Amelia, you're looking real well. I can't get over
how you never look any older."

"Ha."

"It's true. Now that you're really famous I would
think that the years would start to show."

"I'm not that famous." She smiled. "When I *am* recognized, I'm usually mistaken for somebody else."

"No, you're famous. And I never thought anything
of it when you became so well known. From the time
I was two or three, I think even my earliest memory,
you were around the house singing. I knew you were
great even then. And then you were gone, and your
records started coming out."

"There's a lot of time you don't mention. The coffee-
houses and small clubs. I miss a little of that intimacy,
but there sure wasn't any money in those days. I wish
we were closer in age, because when I quit school and
left home I missed you growing up. I sort of made you
an only child very early on, didn't I? It was kind of
rough on the family, I guess. I thought Daddy hated me
for dropping out of school."

"He never hated you," Leaner said.

"I know. When I visited him in the hospital before he...before the end, the first album had just come out." Amelia shaded her eyes and cleared her throat, and her voice grew a little unsteady. "Sorry. I told him then that I shouldn't have left home like that. That at the time I thought I knew what was good for me better than he did. He managed to turn on his side, and he flipped on this little record player by the bed, and it was me singing. I don't recall his exact words. He said something about how songbirds are too pretty to keep in cages. 'And I couldn't be prouder of my nightingale,' he said. It was a Father Knows Best sentiment, but I went to pieces, and he held me in his arms." She folded her hands in her lap and looked out over the meadow. "I dream about Daddy sometimes," she said. "Mom, too."

Leaner brushed away a tear from his sister's cheek. "So do I," he said.

"Some Indian tribes used to believe that the spirits of the dead visit you in dreams."

"I had heard that," Leaner said. "It's a nice thought."

Amelia wiped her face with the palms of her hands and threw her hair back. "Thurmond, how in the world did you get involved with professional golf?"

"By accident, at first." Leaner shook his head. "Some guy I knew in college asked me to go along with him once. I took a few shots. He gave me some tips, and I was amazed at how the shots improved just during that first day. It was fun. You know, just the accomplishment of driving a ball. So I borrowed his clubs a few times, then I bought my own. This guy had been playing since he was ten or so, but within a couple of weeks

I was beating him. I started playing in a few amateur tournaments, then last year I won one of them in Texas."

"That was at Lake Something-or-other, wasn't it?"

"Lake Baldy. I've no idea where that name came from. So after I won that, and qualified as a pro this year, I was invited to play in the Catskills."

"I know you put a lot of work into it," Amelia said. "Music is all I've wanted as far as a career goes, and I'm satisfied with where I've gotten. Most people with the same goal never make it. Luck has something to do with it, but a lot of people want it all at once. Take you, for instance. How many golfers dream of turning pro but don't understand that in addition to the talent there's a hell of a lot of hard work? My rehearsing, your practice, can be boring. It's enough to make you scream sometimes. But look at the end result."

"Oh, sure, you have to work at it. But you know, Amelia, there's something about the game I can't put my finger on. When you know where you want to place a shot, and you hit it just like you know you have to, and the ball takes off into the air, you know you've made the shot before it's even landed. You've done your homework and it's paid off. But it's more than that. There's an excitement to slamming the ball in a drive. People don't realize that most good tee shots would be hit out of any baseball stadium. So, in a way, every time you hit a drive you're hitting a home run. A lot of guys don't like the putting, it takes so much concentration, but when the ball drops in the hole and hits solidly in the bottom of the cup, there's this surge of energy. I like the independence of golf, too. In team sports you always have to rely on someone else doing their job. And golf isn't like boxing or tennis, where you're one-on-one. Mostly, you play yourself, plus the course. It's unique."

"Are you hard on yourself?"

"It doesn't do any good to throw your club into a pond or smack it against a tree. If a shot doesn't go the way I want it to, it's not the ball's fault, or the club's. I've done something wrong, and I try to correct it. Sometimes you can't figure out what it is, and it drives you crazy. You need outside help then. If you're lucky a minor adjustment is all it takes. Does any of this make any sense?"

"Yes, it does.... You have a head on your shoulders, little brother. Oh, while I'm thinking about it, if things don't work out to your liking in New York, or even if they do, my agent is in Boston. He mainly does commercials, and he uses athletes quite a bit. Why don't you look him up on your way home? I can let him know that you're coming."

"I don't know," Leaner said. "I'm not the famous member of the family."

"Thurmond, you don't have to be. Anyway, it'll give you an excuse to see Boston, if nothing else."

Leaner pictured himself on television, berating a make-believe spouse's floor polish. Then, switching scenes after an absolutely effortless sponge mopping, staring at his reflection in acrylic tile, a contented man.

"I guess it won't hurt to have his name."

"By the way, there's something I wanted to get done before lunch. It takes some lifting."

'Sure."

"There was something else, if I can remember.... Oh, yes. I don't have a telephone right now. Charles was playing with it yesterday. He's always taking things apart. The problem is, he doesn't always get them back in one piece. He's pretty embarrassed by it. Anyway, if you have to make a call you'll have to go out to a pay phone. I'll pick up a new phone when I go to town next. They sell them in the grocery store now. Can you believe it?"

Suddenly Leaner could think of nothing to say, but fortunately his sister just assumed that he was enjoying a lazy peaceful morning like she was. He downed the dregs of the coffee, feeling the liquid squeeze past a knot forming somewhere between his stomach and throat. He managed a grin for Amelia, one that he was sure made him appear guilty of a petty crime. It was, of course, anxiety. This tournament was more than golf. It was Leaner at last taking a chance on himself, accepting the challenge of it. That was what made the knot.

Noises from the woods on the far side of the meadow were a welcome diversion, and Leaner spotted his niece and nephew moving out from the shade into the open expanse of the meadow. They had a graceful gait that give the impression of cross-country skiing, their leg movements obscured by tall grass. It was more a glide than a walk, and Leaner pegged it as a lanky but graceful back-east strut. The two children waved in unison, and Leaner returned their greeting with a salvo of his own. "Ahoy!" he shouted. They waved once more, and Leaner continued his salutation until he could nearly bend over the porch railing and pat them on the head.

"How y'all doing?"

"Fine," they both answered.

Leaner smiled at them, wondering how different his

life might have been if he and Amelia had been twins.

"Where'd you go?" he asked.

Charles did a little foot-kicking routine before speaking, a standing shuffle he seemed to be patenting. Leaner guessed that he was bashful.

"We just went walking," he said. "Followed the creek, then climbed a hill. Then we came back."

"We saw some deer," Jean said. "Mom, I'm thirsty."

"I think there's water left in the kitchen," Amelia told her.

She went inside a minute later and called for the children to wash up for lunch. Leaner opened the sliding glass door for his niece and nephew. After they had seated themselves, Amelia asked Leaner if there was anything in particular he would like to do during his visit.

"Not really," he said, all traces of the lump having vanished. "Don't go out of your way just to show me around."

Charles had been tapping his feet beneath the table, waiting for a blank spot in the conversation, and jumped right in when he saw his chance.

"Uncle Thurmond, can you teach me how to juggle?"

"What has your mother been telling you?" Leaner said. "I can't juggle."

"That was Cousin Rose," Amelia said.

"I don't know any Cousin Rose, either."

"You'll meet her tomorrow at the reunion," Amelia said, then smacked her forehead with the palm of her hand. "I forgot to tell you. I've planned a family reunion here tomorrow. It turns out that the countryside is full of Leaners."

Leaner put his sandwich down. "Just a minute," he

said. "We're both from Texas. I didn't know there were any more of us anywhere else."

"Mother," Charles interrupted, "we have finished our delicious meal and it is imperative that my sister and I search for newts near the spring. May we please be excused?"

"If it's *imperative*, go ahead," Amelia said, and they flew from the table. "I've been working on their manners," she explained. "Twelve is some age, you know? Anyway, yes, Thurmond. We are from Texas, but our grandfather left this area of Pennsylvania as a young man. We're just the offshoot of the family down there. A few Leaners left to work in the oil fields when oil was discovered there. Before that, they built wooden derricks near Drake Well. That was the first oil discovery in North America. About an hour's drive from here. Are you with me so far?"

"I think so."

"And our grandfather's grandfather—would he be our great-great grandpappy?—anyway, he was the first Leaner in the United States. He had a lot of kids, and so did those kids. So we have tons of distant relatives all over the place up here."

"Why didn't I know this?"

"I don't know. Daddy never talked much about it. I don't know that Mother ever had it all clear.... Before they begin to arrive tomorrow I'd like to have the driveway lined with logs to keep the cars out of the flowerbeds."

Leaner finished his sandwich, trying not to be obvious as he looked at his sister, wondering whether it was a family trait that made Amelia look so young, if Leaners had some sort of Shangri-La edge on aging that had bypassed the general populace. How his sister could be famous and still look so *normal* amazed him.

"How do you handle it?" he asked. "Being famous, I mean."

"In stages," she said. "The music business can be dehumanizing, and I was insecure about a lot of things, mainly having an image. The image may or may not be a true one, but the public tends to look at you in those terms. The worst thing, the absolute worst, about all of it is when a total stranger declares his love for you. That's a little frightening. What I did was to marry when I was insecure, and divorce when I saw it wasn't a loving relationship anymore. I try to put the kids first, and there's this place in the woods. I like the isolation and the slow pace. Mainly, it's the kids."

"I guess having a family makes all the difference," Leaner said. "You know what I think is funny is that all the articles I've seen on you almost automatically mention your name in connection with Joni Mitchell and Emmylou Harris."

"It's a sort of convenience for writers to lump people together. I know Emmylou. I like her a lot. Joni Mitchell, I haven't met. I usually like their stuff, though, but saying we three are the same is making us interchangeable.

A hundred yards from the road was an area of dead pines. Some were fallen, and those left standing were without limbs. They had been dead for some time, and Leaner found that the ones on the ground were too rotted to suit their purposes. He and Amelia took turns pushing on the trunks of the standing ones until they had a nice pile of driveway liners. The children lent support by hanging around, kicking bushes and tossing rocks here and there.

"Did you catch any newts?" Leaner asked them.

"Two," Jean said.

"What did you do with them?"

"We tagged them and let them go," Charles said.

Leaner judged that the logs were roughly the size of four-by-fours. He hoped that Amelia was more coordinated than he in carrying them. He tended to be downright clumsy with physical labor, although he was precise in taking measurements and careful in his work—which made him a good construction worker in spite of the bumper crop of bruises that he raised.

They hoisted a ten-footer into the air, tucking it beneath their arms like a battering ram. It was immediately evident that Amelia shared his handicap, another family characteristic, as they carried the tree trunk slightly uphill with groans and stubbed toes.

3

LEANER HURRIED TO THE
car and, without bothering to turn around, backed up
the four hundred yards to the road, scraping bushes
along the way, nearly losing control once in loose gravel.
He made a contrail of red dust as he raced down the
iron ore road, the large branches looming overhead
breaking the sunlight into a radiant series of strobo-
scopic flashes. The sound of rocks bouncing off the
underside of his vehicle seemed thunderous....

On his second morning Leaner had allowed himself
a carton of yogurt while his relatives had a more con-
ventional and fulfilling breakfast. After the meal the
group was a portrait of leisure. Charles and Jean were
outside somewhere, and Leaner was talking with Amelia as she prepared for the family reunion. She had asked
Leaner during small talk how Lauren was, and he almost choked on the question. He had completely forgotten to call her when he had safely reached Amelia's.
"Quick, where's the nearest phone?" he had asked, and
ran to his car.

Now he hit his brakes and skidded sideways. "What's the hurry?" he said. "I'm a day late as it is."

He followed Amelia's directions and breezed through Cyclone toward Kane, the slower speed calming him enough to keep an eye open for signs of a public telephone, though Amelia had warned him that there might not be one for miles.

At the peak of a small hill the forest opened to reveal a small building with a dirt parking lot, a bar, maybe a place where lumberjacks hung out, throwing down boilermakers one by one, making life hell for any stranger who might walk inside.

He made for the front door, imagining having to win an ax-throwing contest before earning the right to use the telephone. He opened the door; it was so dark inside that he had to let his eyes adjust for a moment. It was like walking in on the middle of a movie. It was only a small bar, with two accompanying tables. There weren't, he noted with some relief, any huge types in the place. He noticed that the phone on the wall was already tied up so he pulled out the only available stool and ordered a beer, eavesdropping on the conversation around him while sneaking a glance at the phone now and then.

"You shoulda seen her," the man at Leaner's side was telling his companion. "Great titties, and what a pair of legs. Long perfect legs. A hundred miles of her."

The other one started up now. "That's nothing. South Philly. Last New Year's. Not New Year's Eve. New Year's Day. I was waiting for my bus and these two broads pulled up and offered me a ride. *Two* of them."

Leaner pulled on his beer.

"Did you go with them?"

"Did I go with them? Is that what you're asking me? What the hell do you think? Ten minutes later we were at their place, and they had my pants down. Funny thing was, they turned out to be dykes."

"Couple of lezzies, huh?"

"Oh, yeah. But they both sucked me off anyway before going after each other. I guess they sort of warmed up on me."

Leaner pushed himself away from the bar and went to stand right behind the man using the phone to see if that would hurry him up. He really wanted to get back to Amelia's and not upset her by arriving late for the reunion. "Excuse me," he finally said, "I'd like to use the phone when you get off. I'll use it, then get right on out of here."

"In a minute, Bud. I'm almost through," he said, then spoke into the receiver. "Some nut's waiting to use the phone. Why don't I just come on over tonight. Yeah. Yeah. Bye." He hung up. "It's all yours, Bud."

Leaner thought briefly how surprised the man would have been to catch a beer bottle across the bridge of his nose. He really disliked being called Bud, with a vengeance.

Over the phone it sounded as if there was already a conversation going in full swing....

"Get down from there!" Lauren was shouting. "Get down and come here! Oh, just a minute."

He heard the receiver fall to the floor, bouncing with a tubular echo.

"Sorry," Lauren finally said. "Can I help you?"

"Collect call from Thurmond Leaner."

"I'll accept. Thurmond, so you're not lying in a ditch somewhere. Where have you been—? God *damn* it, *stop* it."

"Who are you talking to? Has the dog gone crazy?"

"It's a long story," Lauren said. "I was a little anxious yesterday when you didn't call, so I went out for a drive and ended up at the pet store where I'd bought the dog's flea collar. I'd seen a monkey there, and on impulse I bought him, and now he won't hold still and let me measure him for a little western outfit I want to make him. In fact, I was having a hell of a time getting him down off the refrigerator when you called. Do monkeys bite?"

"Of course they bite," Leaner said. "They bite, they have fleas, they masturbate, piss and shit. They are not cute after looking at them with a sane eye for ten minutes. What possessed you to do such a thing?"

"Hey, pardon me," Lauren said. "I thought I was capable of decisions. The store owner's a real nice man, and he convinced me that the dog was digging because he was lonely. He suggested that the monkey would be the perfect little companion for backyard expeditions. I'm making a cowboy outfit for him, and somewhere I'm going to find a miniature saddle for the dog. And if you don't like it, that's just too bad for you, because I'm not getting rid of Bingo."

Leaner's ears felt hot, and if he looked into a mirror it wouldn't surprise him to see his hair standing on end.

"Lauren," he said, "please take the monkey back."

"You'd never say that if you saw him eat a banana. It's a scream, Thurmond. A *scream*. I already told you I can't get rid of him. It's just something you'll have

to live with, Thurmond, listen to me. I don't want to
be with anyone but you. This is just an eccentricity,
and it really isn't that out of character, is it? Were you
that surprised when I told you?"

"No, but that doesn't mean I wanted to hear it.
Lauren, I've got to get back to Amelia's. Her phone's
been knocked out, by the way. I just wanted to tell you
I've made it here in one piece. I want you to do something for me. I want you to ask yourself, 'Can I live
with this monkey on my back?'"

"You mean one more monkey."

If he had been transported to the reunion at the
moment he'd hung up, he just might have knocked the teeth out of the first relative he encountered....
"A real nice man convinced me to buy a monkey,"
he said aloud in the car. "I'll bet he never took his
eyes off her legs, either. I don't want anyone but you.
When you're here, no doubt. But in the meantime, the
monkey salesman'll do. Hi. Remember me? I sold
you the monkey. I saw your address on the check, and
was in the neighborhood. How is Bingo adjusting to
his new home. ... ?"

What's the matter with me? Don't I love Lauren?
Don't I trust her? And so what if she has a discreet
transgression that's only physical? What's the big deal?
He turned in the driveway. Still, if she's fooling around,
who's to say I'd be out of line to have a fling myself?
If I felt like it...

He had to park well away from the house because
the guests were already arriving, then managed to make
it through the living room and up the stairs undetected.
After changing clothes he found himself in the kitchen

with Amelia as she put the finishing touches on a number of snack trays.

"Here, stir this," she told him, plopping a bowl in his hands. "I've got to finish these trays."

Leaner guessed that he was mixing a cake of some kind. It was an orange batter with some blue-colored berries thrown in. Just as he was about to sample it, Amelia snatched it away. "I said to stir it, not beat it to death."

"I'll just go out on the porch," he said.

Leaner could see Charles in the meadow walking a few people around, pointing here and there. He sat next to his niece. "Jean, which one of you is older, you or Charles?"

"He's older," she said. "But I'm bigger. He's a shrimp."

"That's not a very nice thing to say about your brother."

"Well, he is. Where were you? We picked some berries while you were gone."

"I had to go find a telephone and tell everyone at home that I'm all right. What kind of berries?"

"They're like blueberries, only not so big. We wanted you to pick some with us."

"Maybe tomorrow we can. I want to hit a few balls around. We could go after the berries at the same time maybe. Does that sound okay?"

"You know what?" Jean said. "Well, there's an old power line or something over the hill. There's almost no trees, and it looks like a golf course, sort of, because it's real narrow. We can show it to you, and there's berry patches there too."

"That sounds fine," Leaner said.

Charles was leading his group back to the house.

They were all middle-aged—fifties, sixties and older. They didn't seem to resemble each other, or Leaner, any more than a random crowd of pedestrians in a shopping mall would.

"This is Mom's brother Thurmond Leaner," Charles said. "You can introduce yourselves, I guess. I might get something wrong."

A small man in his seventies or eighties wearing a red flannel shirt was the first to reach Leaner. "They call me the Kid," he said, slapping Leaner's shoulder with the back of his hand. "Where you from?"

"Houston."

"Sure did come a long way for this get-together, didn't you?"

"No, sir, I was—"

"Call me Kid. Everybody does."

"All right," Leaner said. "Kid. I'm up here visiting with Amelia and *her* kids for a week or so."

"That so?" the Kid said. "I was in Texas during the war. El Paso. You get over to El Paso very often?"

"No, I've never been there," Leaner said. "It's about nine hundred miles from home."

"Nine hundred miles." The Kid pondered. "Big state. Big, big state. Dorothy, come meet 'Melia's brother. He says that Houston is nine hundred miles from El Paso, and I have the suspicion he's telling us the truth. This is my wife Dorothy, Thurmond. We live on the other side of the river."

"How do you do?" Leaner said, feeling very much the center of attention. "I might be wrong about that mileage. It could be only seven hundred."

"How do you come to be a Leaner?" Dorothy asked him.

Below:

"I'm no historian," Leaner said. "Apparently a branch of the family moved south. Are you a Leaner?"

"I used to be, till I married the Kid. I'm a Doolin now. Let's see. If you're Amelia's brother, that means that my father and your grandfather were probably first cousins. So somewhere, way back, we had a common ancestor."

"I suppose so," Leaner said.

No one else seemed to be doing any of the talking, and when Leaner stopped speaking there was dead silence. Finally a fat woman nudged someone else, gesturing at Leaner, saying, "He looks like Doris's Leland."

Leaner excused himself from the company of the Kid and Mrs. Doolin and seated himself beside the woman. "Pardon me," he said. "Did you say that I look like Cloris Leachman?"

The woman threw back her head and laughed a wheezy and tear-filled laugh, jiggling the pouch of fat above her elbows. "Oh, listen to him," she cried. "That's rich. Cloris Leachman."

Leaner chuckled too. Six or eight carloads of relatives were driving up now, and none of them were under sixty years of age. Leaner felt like the envoy of a small, youthful nation, an island with a language of its own, undecipherable to outsiders. Kid Doolin latched onto his arm. "Say, Tex," he said, "what do you use on deer down your way? I favor the thirty-thirty. Breaks right through small tree limbs and puts an animal down in its tracks."

Leaner pretended not to hear the Kid. He excused himself and left the porch to see whether any food was being served yet. The Kid's grasp was tight and leathery, but Leaner managed to pry himself loose. In the kitchen, the cake was cooling on a platter. It had turned green in the oven, and Amelia was complaining about its appearance.

"Cakes shouldn't be green," she said. "I'm not a bit proud of it, but my children wanted to add blueberries to an orange cake, so what could I do?"

"Don't worry about it, Amelia," Leaner said seriously, taking a large slice and stuffing it in his mouth. "It's delicious, and you can save some in the freezer for St. Patrick's Day. Go outside and relax." Ignoring his own advice, he deserted the kitchen and tried the door of the downstairs bathroom. He was locked out. He climbed the flight of stairs to the other bathroom, but it was in use as well. He waited outside the door a minute, then entered the room he was staying in. From the window he could see the assembled Leaner clan. Food was being carried out on paper plates, and makeshift seats were filling up. Leaner surveyed the group from the window. They weren't a bad-looking bunch. He wondered which of the women was Rose, his cousin the juggler. He heard the bathroom door open but stayed at the window, resting his elbows on the sill as he peered about.

The Kid was sitting in a chair and looking into the air as if he were watching a flight of high-altitude geese. He may have been studying the clouds. Suddenly he spotted Leaner in the window and leaped from his seat, pointing.

"There he is!" he shouted. "Whatcha doing up there, Tex?"

"I'm just thinking," Leaner called back.

"What about, Tex?"

Leaner was imagining his backyard at home, wondering whether Lauren was transforming it into a practice arena for Bingo and the dog. He didn't want to go into it with Kid Doolin at the moment. "Just thinking," Leaner repeated.

He moved away from the window and went to the bathroom. When he was washing up, there was a knock on the door. "Just a minute," he said, looking at himself in the mirror while toweling his hands dry. He found a brush and ran it through his hair. When he finished he held back the hair above his forehead to examine whether the hairline was retreating. This was the first time he had ever done this. It was only an exercise in curiosity, he told himself. He had no anxiety about growing old. He opened the door, and Amelia was standing there with her arms crossed.

"What's the matter?" she asked. "Was there bad news from home? I didn't even ask."

"She bought a monkey, Amelia. It's probably shitting on my pillow by now."

Leaner almost immediately regretted using an obscenity in front of his older sister, then realized that she was not offended in the least. She was accustomed to such language, he thought, being involved in the music industry.

"So you're all right, then," she said. "I saw you in the window and heard that cryptic statement you made."

"I didn't mean to be cryptic, Amelia. Everything is fine."

"Good," Amelia said. She let down her arms and squeezed his hand. "Come get some food before it's all gone."

When he seated himself on the porch, Leaner was

relieved to see that the Kid had found someone else to bombard with his questions and opinions. He was probably a nice little man. Maybe parties fired him up, which was understandable. He waved a friendly chicken wing at the Kid, and the Kid pointed his finger back at him like a pistol, firing off a couple of imaginary shots.

"You're Thurmond?" a man asked.

Leaner tucked some potato salad into his cheek and nodded.

"I'm Vernon Leaner," the man said. "Pleased to meet you."

"Same here," Leaner said. "I was telling Amelia yesterday that I didn't know there were any more Leaners up here. It's very surprising."

"We're not too plentiful anymore," Vernon said, shaking his head. "You probably don't remember this, but I've met you before. I went down to Houston for a funeral."

"Oh, yes, I do remember that. We had you over to the house?"

"That's right. I had dinner with you and your folks." Vernon looked at Leaner. "You know, you've grown."

Leaner laughed, a restrained laugh so as not to offend Vernon. "I was only twelve," he said.

"What do you do for a living?"

"I remodel houses," Leaner said. "And I'm trying to be a pro golfer. My first tournament is in New York in a few days. How about yourself? What do you do?"

"I grow Christmas trees," Vernon told him. "Got about a hundred acres. I tell you, you really have to budget doing something like that. One sale has to last you the whole year. Course, if I wanted to, I could strip-mine my land. A coal company talked to me about it.

They said it's solid coal under the surface. Hell, I already knew that. That's hardly a reason to tear up the land. Not just for money."

"That's admirable," Leaner said. "I mean that."

Heck," Vernon said, "some things you just can't replace. After strip-mining they put the dirt back in the holes or rebuild your hill, but it's not the same. When Amelia bought this property, we worried that she'd sell her coal, but she feels like we do. Some things are just more important. And let me tell you something else. I don't like unions, either. I don't know how you feel about them, but I don't like them. My grandfather worked in a mine around the turn of the century. He pumped air into the shafts. When some of the miners went on strike, he was sympathetic. But he stayed on the job. He couldn't suffocate a man just because he disagreed with him. Anyway, the strikers finally won, and my grandfather was blacklisted. He never worked another day in his life." Vernon emphasized his punch line with squinted eyes and a Walter Brennan nod of affirmation.

"That's awful," Leaner said, pushing away his plate. "I guess what he should have done was to make it clear to everyone else that he didn't know about them, but that the air pump would be out of service until further notice. That might have made up a few minds."

"Wouldn't have worked," Vernon said. "Some martyr would still go down there."

Leaner found the conversation increasingly depressing. Vernon went on from the mining story to more tales of destitution, disease and hard luck. Most of the incidents didn't even occur to people Vernon knew. He usually prefaced a tragedy with, "I heard about this family in Kentucky..." or, "There was this thing in a magazine I saw..."

"...so he was found innocent, but meanwhile he'd spent fourteen years at hard labor. Legal fees and court costs would keep him broke for the rest of his life, which he ended by drowning himself in a bathtub."

"What can I say?" Leaner said. "Life can be tough."

"You bet it can," punctuated again with that squint and nod.

Leaner looked around for some way to escape Vernon's company before being convinced to slash his wrists out of sympathy for a particularly horrible event. He picked up his plate and carried his scraps to the kitchen. Amelia was there laughing with a guest and threw her arm around him as he was walking by. "Tell me the truth," she said to the woman. "Do my brother and I look like each other?"

"Well, yes," the woman said. "Around the eyes especially. You both have those youthful Leaner good looks. You could even be the same age, but I know better."

"How old are you?" Leaner asked his sister.

She smiled. "The name should give it away. Daddy was not so secretly in love with Amelia Earhart. As a public figure, you understand, and I was named after her. Maybe that's not such a hint, because I *was* born ages after her plane crashed."

"Oh, yes. That was back in my day, Amelia."

"I'm forty," Amelia said. "You dragged it out of me. The big four-oh. Tell Thurmond what you were telling me about the origin of the family name."

"There are a couple of theories," the woman said. "One is that our noble ancestor had an unpronounceable German name, and after a game of horseshoes, he was given the name Leaner. A leaner is when the horseshoe just leans on the stake. It's not a complete miss, in other words."

"That's pretty hard to swallow," Leaner said.

"Yeah? Tell it to the Ringers. Another story is that our namesake got into an argument with a butcher over the quality of the meat. Seems the butcher was giving him too much fat, and in his broken English, our ancestor kept yelling, 'Leaner! Leaner!'"

"That's no better," Leaner said.

"I agree," the woman said. "Theory Number Three. We found some old letters once, and the name on the envelopes was Loehner. L-o-e-h-n-e-r. The name was changed to sound more American."

"I'll go with that," Leaner said.

Dorothy Doolin rushed in to the kitchen now, looking flushed and frantic.

"Have you see the Kid?" she asked. "No one outside has seen him for half an hour. Is he in here?"

"He must be," Amelia assured her. "Thurmond, get Dorothy a glass of water. I'll look through the house."

Leaner filled a coffee mug from the tap, and Dorothy sat down at the table with it. "This just isn't like the Kid," she said. "He's too fond of people to go off by himself. Oh, what if he's wandered away and gotten himself lost or hurt?"

Vernon came in now and asked about the Kid just as Amelia was descending the stairs, shaking her head. Leaner saw Vernon's eyes squint and knew that bad news was on the way.

"This happened to a fellow in Yellowstone once," Vernon said. "He got torn apart by bears."

Dorothy Doolin burst into tears.

Word spread quickly of the Kid's disappearance. The children made a fruitless search of the vehicles in the driveway. People were milling about everywhere, and when Charles and Jean reported their news to the household that the Kid was not asleep in one of the cars, Dorothy Doolin could be heard from across the meadow, acting as if the Kid's bear-claw-riddled body had turned up in a clump of brush. A man Leaner hadn't met felt obligated to take charge, and stood on a living room chair to be heard.

"Everyone, may I have your attention?" he was saying. "If you haven't already heard, Kid Doolin has disappeared. I'm asking anyone who feels up to it to start a search. If you're not familiar with the property, it's easy to lose your sense of direction. That's probably what happened to the Kid. He's just a little turned around out there and needs some help coming home. I would like most of you to stay here. There's no need for more of us to get lost. If the Kid shows up while we're out in the woods, start honking the car horns so we'll know he's safe. This is not a crisis, and that may bear repeating." The man waited a moment, studying the group. "This is not a crisis."

Dorothy Doolin screamed.

A six-man posse spread out from the house. Leaner and Vernon walked across the meadow together before parting, but it was time enough for Vernon to recollect two additional horror stories, one about a skier who had broken both legs above the knees ten miles from the nearest telephone, covering the distance in three days by pulling himself along over rocks and bushes hand over hand, mile by mile. "Then there was that pregnant woman who got raped by that motorcycle gang from Illinois," Vernon told him. "There were about twenty of them, and they acted like a bunch of animals."

"What does that have to do with the Kid?" Leaner asked.

"She miscarried, too," Vernon finished it off. "Just thought you might want to know, that's what."

Leaner found a creek and began to follow a path that ran alongside it. He was only a few yards from the meadow but the house was already obscured from view. The ground was very dry and he wasn't certain that he would be able to recognize any footprints. "Kid," he called out. "Kid Doolin." For some reason Leaner was looking in trees. He wasn't paying close attention to what he was doing, and stepped into the edge of the creek. *Jesus, what am I doing, tromping around in a forest in the Keystone State looking for the ancient husband of a distant relative?* He cupped his hands and shouted as loudly as he could, "Hello, Kid Doo-ooo-lin!" Calling out to the Kid sounded like a song. "Oh, you Ki-i-i-id!"

He was getting so far from the house that he was sure the Kid couldn't have gone such a distance without hearing his calls. He decided to circle back in another direction, noting that if he himself should become lost there would always be the creek to give him his bearings.

He ended up on the iron ore road about a half-mile from the driveway and, giving the Kid credit for taking the easiest route, walked down the middle of it toward the house. He sang out the Kid's name about every ten seconds, but there was never an answer.

As Leaner rounded a curve, he saw him about fifty yards ahead. The Kid was down on his knees and appeared to be clutching his throat. Leaner began to sprint, not really sure what he would do if the Kid was having an attack of some kind. He was already thinking about scooping up the Kid without breaking stride, throwing the little man over his shoulder and whisking him away to the safety of the house. The Kid heard Leaner running toward him and stood up to see what the noise was. Leaner immediately saw that he was fine and nonchalantly slowed to a brisk walk, saying, "Kid Doolin."

"Hey, there, Tex. You look out of breath."

"Everyone's worried about you. You didn't tell a soul where you were going."

"Kid Doolin can take care of himself," he said. "I've just been eating berries. They're best when you pick them right off the bush and pop them in your mouth."

"Your wife is really upset. And I can't say that Vernon put her mind to rest any."

"That Vernon Leaner," the kid sneered as they headed toward the house. "He's a blue-blond horse's ass."

When they turned in the driveway Leaner could hear the cheers from the porch, and car horns began sounding their arrival. A crowd rushed to greet them, led by Dorothy Doolin wiping her running mascara from her cheeks. People were slapping both Leaner and the Kid on their backs. Soon the other searchers had returned, congratulating Leaner with handshakes and smiles.

And, fittingly, very soon thereafter the reunion was over.

4

THE FOLLOWING MORNING
Leaner was overcome by a lethargy that took him by
surprise. It would suit him just fine to stay in bed all
day, dozing now and then, spending his waking hours
watching the breeze blow the curtains above his bed.
He lay on his side, seeing the tops of the trees through
the window, marveling at how the temperature was
like a Texas autumn.

There was a knock at the door, and one of the children asked if he was "up and at 'em" yet. From behind
the door, he couldn't tell if it was the boy or the girl.

"I'm awake," he said, watching the shadow at the
foot of the door.

"When do you think we can go pick berries and practice your golf?"

"I'll be down in a minute," Leaner said.

He helped himself to coffee but passed up breakfast
once again. The conversation in progress centered on
the excitement of the family reunion. Leaner was

drinking his coffee black, but he stirred it around with his spoon anyway.

"It was pretty irresponsible," Amelia was saying. "Even cruel, for the Kid to pull his vanishing act like that. He ought to be ashamed of himself."

Leaner shrugged. "Oh, I don't know," he said. "No harm done, really."

Charles and Jean were waiting outside for Leaner with a couple of Mason jars for the berries. Leaner shouldered his golf bag, and as soon as he was out the door, both children were asking to carry his clubs. Leaner explained to them that the clubs weren't so heavy when you first picked them up, but they could really get to you after a while. "I've been carrying them a long time," he said. "You have to know what you're doing or you'll hurt yourself."

As they climbed a hill spotted with loose ground cover and hip-fracturing gullies, Leaner was thankful that Kid Doolin hadn't meandered over this way. He probably would have broken something, and in addition to whatever misery he might experience as a result of the accident, it would just become more fodder for Vernon's repertoire of horror tales.

"You know what?" Jean said.

"What?" said Leaner.

"We're almost there."

Leaner had to hand it to his young niece and nephew. They certainly knew a good place to hit golf balls. Ancient poles of roughly hewn timber extended to the horizon at the abandoned power line. It was the only unobstructed view of any distance on the property, and it looked perfect for using as a driving range, although scrub brush and small pine seedlings were beginning to reclaim the space.

Leaner took out his driver and teed up a ball. At last he had some time on the trip that he could consider his own.

"Y'all stay over here where you won't catch my backswing. After I hit all of the balls we can go see how many we can find. They're real cheap practice balls, so it doesn't matter how many we lose."

"It's sort of like an Easter egg hunt," Charles said.

"No, it's not," his sister argued. "This is work."

Leaner took a couple of practice swings, hoping to stay within the narrow confines of the right-of-way with his shots. He wasn't famous for his distance, which was only above average—or, as a matter of fact, famous for anything else at this point in his life. But he was an accurate shooter. The path his balls flew was almost always arrow-straight, except when he wanted to fade or draw.

He shifted his weight from one foot to the other like a cat sinking its claws into its favorite rug, then let go with the first drive, and the children were flabbergasted, both of them jumping in place. "Wow!" Charles said. "How far did that go?"

"Six hundred yards," Leaner dead-panned.

"Six hundred yards! Wow!"

"It didn't go half that far," Jean protested. "God, Pee-wee, you believe anything."

"Don't call me Pee-wee," Charles said.

"Here we go again," Leaner said. "Y'all watch."

He was machinelike in his precision, and the youngsters were a great little gallery, squealing and shouting at every shot like they were at a fireworks display. He hit all the balls he had brought with him, and when it was time to shag them the children raced on ahead of him and counted them as they picked them up. Out of the fifty balls, they had found all but six, and when Leaner hit them back the other way, only two more were lost. The reason they were having such an easy time of it was that Leaner placed most of them from the tee within a radius of no more than ten steps. He was very pleased.

Leaner began to use his irons, explaining why there were so many, how each had a different loft used for various combinations of angle and distance and lie. They were attentive but never once asked if they could try out the clubs themselves. Actually they were dying to, but Amelia had earlier laid down the law about keeping their hands off of them.

Just as Leaner was about to hit one of the last balls, an unexpected movement distracted him, and the ball flew out of control into the woods a hundred yards down the line. Three deer the size of mules bolted across the area, followed by a fawn that stopped in the clearing and gave the people its full attention, both ears cocked. Charles waved his arms and yelled, and the fawn leaped into the woods, followed by the other deer.

"Why'd you do that?" Leaner asked him.

"To make him scared of people," he said. "If he stands still like that in November, someone's bound to shoot him."

"Hunters trespass on your land?"

"Yeah, we don't even come up here in the winter. People are all over the place with guns."

Jean had been staring at a point past where the deer

had appeared, in the vicinity of where the golf ball had gone. "Something fell, back in there," she said. "And it was bigger than a tree limb. I saw it go down."

"Well," Leaner said, "let's go have a look."

They walked to the general area and began rooting around, and after a few minutes Charles found the ball. While he was examining it, Jean let out a shriek worthy of Dorothy Doolin.

"Thurmond, come quick!"

Leaner hopped over a couple of logs to see what the daily crisis mill had turned up for him this time. Jean was sitting on the ground cradling the head of an unconscious young man in her lap. "Is he dead, Uncle Thurmond?" she asked, wide-eyed.

Leaner was still a few steps away but was already denying to himself any serious injury to the boy. He bent over him, noticing a huge bump square in the center of his forehead. "He's not dead," he said emphatically. "He's been beaned by a ball, that's all." Leaner lifted each of the eyelids because he'd seen it done so often in the movies. He didn't know what he was supposed to be looking for, and he found the act somehow upsetting, too intimate. The youth was wearing hand-woven clothing, all black, and a yellow straw hat lay nearby. "Do you have any idea who he is?"

"It's Jonah," Charles said. "He lives on the other side of our land."

"What is he? Amish?"

"No, the Amish are about twenty miles from here. He's something like that, though. Look, he's moving."

"Hold still," Leaner told the young man. "Don't try to talk." This was another holdover from the movies.

Jonah pulled his legs up and sat on the ground, massaging his forehead, while Leaner and the two children observed him. "What time is it?" Jonah managed to say.

"Before noon," Leaner said. "How do you feel?"

"Dizzy." Jonah spoke haltingly with a remote, non-descript accent. "What has happened? I was watching you hit the balls with those rods of yours. Then some deer ran before me. I saw them run away. Now I find myself on the ground."

"They're not rods," Jean spoke out. "They're called clubs. Golf clubs. And the balls are golf balls. You got hit by one of them."

Leaner nodded apologetically.

"So that is the golf," Jonah said. "I have a radio, and once listened to the golf over it."

Charles nudged his sister, whispering "He's pretty nutty," and they both giggled.

"Try and stand up," Leaner told him. "I'll take you home. It's the least I can do after beaning you."

"Beaning?" Jonah asked.

"It's my fault you're hurt," Leaner said, lifting the boy's arm over his shoulder. "Let's get to my car."

Jonah pulled himself away. "No automobiles," he said. "They are against our beliefs." He then became silent. Occasionally he stumbled, but his walk was steady. Leaner, carrying his bag by its shoulder strap, was ready to catch Jonah should he fall. He felt miserable.

"What lousy luck," he said.

"I must go home," said Jonah. "I have sinned, and this awful thing is my punishment. I must go home."

"What'd he say?" Jean asked.

"He could be delirious, or have a slight concussion,"

Leaner told her. "Don't put too much stock in what he says right now."

Just as their feet stepped onto the road, Jonah swooned dramatically, toppling Leaner and his clubs. Leaner picked him up fireman-style, thinking he might throw out his back in the process, be washed up as a pro before he even got started. Charles immediately picked up the golf bag. It was a real effort for the youngster.

"Hey, Thurmond," Jean said. "If Jonah dies, are they going to arrest you for murder? I mean, we saw you do it. I know it was an accident, but you never can tell what a jury will say."

"Jean," Leaner said, "will you carry this kid's hat for me? It keeps scraping on my neck."

"I'll carry it," she said. "What do they call someone that helps a killer kill somebody?"

"An accessory after the fact," Leaner said. "And if you keep asking me stuff like that, I'm going to start laughing and drop him."

Back at the house, Leaner opened the car door with his free hand and laid Jonah out in the back seat. The children were already screaming the news to Amelia, who got into the car with them as Leaner started the engine. "We've got to get this kid to a hospital," he said, "and X-ray that head of his." As he drove off it occurred to him that his life path had hit rocky ground somewhere in Florida, which was where he had tried for five years to qualify as a professional golfer. Ultimately he had made it, but the Sunshine State was fixed in his mind as a threatening terrain and he never wanted to go back there. Now just about every snag he fell into was linked in his mind with Florida.

When they were a couple of miles down the road, Jonah began to stir in the back seat. He sat up, clenching the armrest as if he were bracing for a ride aboard a Saturn rocket.

"Anyway," Leaner was saying to Amelia, "Jean said she saw something fall in the woods, and we found this fellow knocked out. I came close to hitting a spectator in a tournament once, but never imagined such a thing in an out-of-the-way place like this. I mean, the odds..."

Amelia looked over her shoulder to the back seat. "Did the kids tell you anything about him?"

"Just his name,"

"I bought a quilt from his family. They really do nice work, and some of the men make beautiful furniture. I'm surprised that he was so far from home. Sometimes that group of his, and the Amish as well, encourage the younger ones to raise a little hell to get it out of their systems. He was probably rebelling a bit, going off by himself like that."

"What were you doing so far from home?" Leaner asked into the rear-view mirror.

"I was taking a walk when I should have been working the field."

"He was just taking a walk," Amelia repeated, as if a translation had been called for. "Well, I don't know what they think of modern medical practices. They have a cut-off date of about 1850. Any technology in service up to that point is fine and dandy. You're right, though. He needs X-raying."

They drove into the emergency entrance of the clinic in Kane and assisted Jonah out of the car. He could walk by himself but still had quite a knot on his face. The children stayed in the car. Leaner was the first one in the building and approached a nurse at a desk. "Head X-ray, no insurance, cash payment."

His terse delivery seemed to work. Jonah was led to a back room, Amelia going along with him. Leaner pulled out some traveler's checks. "I'm sorry," the nurse said. "We absolutely cannot accept that as payment. Now, if you were covered by some form of hospitalization or accident benefits—"

"Oh, come on," Leaner said, "the bank must already be closed. These things are as good as cash."

"Not here, they're not," the nurse said firmly.

Amelia was at the desk now. "They want to examine him alone," she said. "Any problem here?"

"They won't take my traveler's check," Leaner complained.

"You're joking," Amelia said, looking at the nurse. "Is Doctor Clark on duty today? He'll take my brother's check."

Something struck a responsive chord in the nurse, and she nearly tore the bill from Leaner's grasp. Leaner assumed that Clark must be a local medical bigwig, and while he wasn't that fond of name-dropping, he had to admit it had its advantages. He wished Amelia would try it again. Maybe that would knock a few bucks off the total.

An intern approached them from down the hall. "Good news," he said. "There's no evidence of a fracture, but he probably has a mild concussion. The boy should get a couple of days rest."

"Where is he now?" Amelia asked him.

"Getting his clothes on," the intern said. "He'll be out in a moment."

Leaner was wondering why the boy had to undress

for a head X-ray, and thought of the time he had gone to an unfamiliar doctor for a school physical and been made to strip to his socks and shoes. After checking only Leaner's ears, the doctor had told him, "That'll be all for today." While Leaner was pulling on his pants he asked the doctor if he had enjoyed himself. "Yes and no," the doctor had shot back, "and be careful how you talk."

"Say," the intern said after studying Amelia. "You're on television, aren't you? You're in that series about the ocean liner?"

"No," Amelia said, folding her arms as she looked down the hall. "Here he comes. Over here, Jonah. We'll take you home."

It was a good thirty-minute drive over to Jonah's community. Jonah had protested that he really shouldn't be riding in a car, but Leaner suggested to him that it might be part of his punishment. Charles and Jean were old hands as car passengers, but they were impressed by the farm they were entering. A hillside and pasture had been cleared by generations past, and a compound of buildings surrounded a central windmill. Leaner looked at the ancient barn, doubting that he could be up to duplicating such a structure if one of his house remodeling jobs ever called for it. Some men and women were working a fine field of crops with hand tools, and one could be seen plowing behind a horse. They were all dressed in simple black or gray, the men wearing stiff white straw hats like Jonah's, the women covering their heads with scarfs. Leaner drove almost to the front door of one building, where an old man with a flowing white beard was sharpening the blade of a scythe. He looked like he was posing for a Quaker Oats cereal box.

"That's grandfather," Jonah said.

"He looks like Father Time," said Leaner, catching Amelia's elbow in his ribs.

The grandfather stood and walked toward the car. Jonah fumbled with the handle to the door on his side of the car, but became so frustrated by it that he climbed out the window.

"Look at him," Jean said. "I can't believe he did that. Boy!"

"Excuse me, sir," Leaner addressed the man. "Jonah had an accident a few miles from here. He was hit on the head, and we took him to the hospital in Kane. The doctor said he should rest up for a few days. I got him a soft drink, and he already looks much better. So maybe he should just stay in bed, listen to his radio and relax."

"Thank you for returning him," the man said before accompanying his grandson inside.

Amelia was shaking her head as they drove slowly from the farm.

"That was some little speech you made there, Thurmond," she said. "I know your intentions were good, but you shouldn't have mentioned the drink and the radio. These people are very strict. It's frivolous for one of them even to turn up the brim of his hat. It's a form of bragging. And God forbid that they should sanction lying around listening to the radio. Oh, well."

"Maybe that isn't the life for Jonah," Leaner said.

"He might leave," Amelia said. "He's about the right age for it. That group of his, I can never remember the name of it, anyway, they have a lot of things that make sense. They have voluntary baptism at the age of twenty-one. That's a good idea. Something like that ought to be a decision rather than being forced on a baby."

"Does that mean we don't have to go to church this Sunday?" Charles asked from the rear.

Amelia didn't answer him. "I've heard that most of the youngsters come back on their own anyway, after a taste of the outside."

"I can't say as I entirely blame them," Leaner said.

5

LEANER ACCOMPANIED AMELIA
and the kids to town the following morning. They were
running low on groceries. The remoteness of Amelia's
property was a mixed blessing to Leaner. He enjoyed
the sounds and sights of nature, but it occurred to him
that maybe he was getting a touch too much of it. The
trip to Kane mixed in a little welcome variety. Besides,
he needed to call home.

He saw a newsstand and bought a copy of the *New
York Times*, tucking it under his arm. He always felt
more at ease about browsing in a place if he had already
bought some of its merchandise, in case a clerk gave
him a hard time about just hanging around. There were
a few books inside, predominantly of local interest. He
noticed a proliferation of pamphlets such as *A History
of the Alleghenies: The Forest and the Mountains*,
Kane's Historic Past and Promising Future, and *Down
the River and Up the Creek—Tall Tales and Outright
Lies*. Invariably, when there was a picture of the author
on the back cover it was of a bearded old man in buck-

skins and horn-rimmed glasses. On shelves, he took a quick look at various Allegheny knick-knacks: pine cone windmills, corncob log cabins and dishes, and ashtrays with maps of Pennsylvania's raw materials.

He returned outside and was about to go over to a bench with his paper when the headline of a tabloid on the newsstand caught his eye. In bold three-inch letters he read: ELVIS SECRET FATHER OF CARO-LINE AND JFK JR??? He couldn't pass by without glancing at the article. There was a photo of Elvis looking back over his shoulder at the photographer, his arm around a woman who could have been anyone. Leaner scanned the story, which said in effect that no, the king of rock-'n'-roll was not the father in question.

He sat down on the bench and opened the *Times*, concentrating on the sports section, weeding it out from the rest and spreading it out on his lap. He tried to find some mention in the paper of the approaching tournament in the Catskills, and was about to give up when, near some Florida jai-alai scores, there was the sentence: "The Catalina Invitational Golf Classic will begin Thursday in Roscoe." Leaner was thrilled that the *New York Times* would take note of the site of his professional debut.

He folded the paper, replacing the sports section. Then, seeing a telephone across the street, he decided that it was as good a time as any to give Lauren a call. While waiting on the corner for the traffic light to change, he felt a wave of nausea and vowed to himself to start a program of common-sense breakfasts instead of skipping that most important meal or, even worse, scarfing down a dozen chocolate cookies as he had that morning. The cookie splurge reminded him of when his maternal grandfather had taken him and a boyhood friend named Paul Matt to see Warren Spahn. It was ages ago, and Houston's minor league team, the Buffs, had folded. The stadium was torn down and in its place was an enormous furniture store. A plaque set into the floor commemorated the spot of the old home plate, which was where Warren Spahn was signing autographs. But on the way home Paul Matt had vomited chocolate cookies all over the back seat of the cavernous old Buick.

Nausea past and present had its effect as Leaner lifted the receiver, and dropped in his coins and reached Directory Assistance in Houston. "Do you have a listing for Paul Matt?" he asked. He was given a number and, being low on change, decided to call collect. A child answered and was struck dumb upon hearing the operator's voice. Finally a man came to the phone.

"Will you accept a collect call from Thurmond Leaner?"

"Who?" Paul Matt asked.

"Leaner. Thurmond Leaner."

There was a long pause. "Oh, sure. Put him on."

"Paul?" Leaner said.

"Hey, Leaner, what's going on?" Even when they were seven-year-olds, Paul Matt had called Leaner by his surname. "Where are you?"

"I'm in Kane, Pennsylvania," Leaner said.

"God, I haven't heard from you in at least fifteen years. What are you up to these days?"

"Oh, you know," Leaner said. "Making a buck here and there. I have something to ask you."

"Is it a legal question?" Paul Matt said. "I'm an attorney now, you know."

"No, I didn't know," Leaner said. "Congratulations on passing the bar. This may sound funny, but do you remember when my grandfather took us to see Warren Spahn?"

"Oh, at that furniture store on the Gulf Freeway. Sure."

"And you threw up on the back seat."

"Yeah."

"I was just wondering," Leaner said. "Why didn't you stick your head out of the window when you knew you were going to be sick?"

"For God's sake, Leaner, I guess I just didn't think of it at the time."

"That's all I wanted to know, Paul. Thanks."

"Yeah, sure...Good luck, Leaner."

That was one of the things Learner loved about the telephone system. A free nationwide information service could put him in touch with almost anyone, even a voice from his past like Paul Matt, now a chocolate-barfing courtroom performer. He took a deep breath. Ready or not, here I come. He got hold of the operator again, though he knew he could dial the number himself.

"I'd like to make a collect call to 713 488-0499."

"And who's calling?"

"Thurmond Leaner, and I realize I could do the dialing. I just didn't feel like it."

"Fine with me, *sir*. I get paid by the hour whatever I do."

It rang eight or nine times before Lauren answered. He could just imagine her chasing the monkey all over the house.

"Yes, I'll accept," she told the operator.

"Hello, Lauren," Leaner said. "It's great to hear your voice."

"You want to know what I did after the last time you called?" Lauren asked. Not waiting for his reply, she went right on. "I broke down and cried like a baby. You made me feel like dirt. I went into the kitchen, took a frozen pie out and put it in the oven. When it was done I polished off half of it in one sitting and finished it for breakfast the next morning. Then I asked myself, 'What am I feeling so down about? He hasn't even met Bingo, and as soon as he does, that little hairy cowboy will melt his heart.' Meanwhile I've put on six pounds, because the pie and other goodies were in addition to three meals a day. I'm not about to give up food."

Leaner was cringing. He had heard Lauren like this once before. It was while they were watching a TV game show in bed. She had started screaming at the set, carrying on about how stupid the contestants were to put up with the shenanigans of the host. She really had the ability to take a thought and run with it.

"What kind of pie?"

"Pecan, with vanilla ice cream piled on it. So you were probably wondering, and I'll tell you, the dog and Bingo hit it off like peaches and cream. I've got the pants and chaps already made out of some spare material and carpet scraps. The tricky part will be finding a saddle for the dog. I've been to a couple of flea markets. No luck. One guy's keeping an eye peeled for me, though. He'll call if anything comes up. It was kind of hard explaining just what I needed, you know? He asked me what kind of dog Business was, then wanted to know why a dog needed a saddle, so I had to tell him about Bingo and all that. I was thinking that maybe a rodeo or something would pay good money just for Bingo to ride across the arena. How much do you think I should charge?"

"You can probably name your price," Leaner told her.

"It's something to think about," she said. "Could you hold on a minute? I've got some cookies ready to come out of the oven."

Leeaner began to daydream about extending his trip, hoping that he would have enough winnings from the tournament to be in no hurry to return to Houston. At the same time, of course, having this urge made him a little ashamed of himself.

"You there?" Lauren said. "There aren't that many cookies. I started eating the dough after it was mixed and nearly put it away. I didn't think you'd be calling today. I guess you missed old Lauren, huh? Well, don't worry about me. I'm holding down the fort on this end, and if everything falls into place, my income with Bingo will help the budget. Oh, I almost forgot. Doctor Mobud phoned. He said that the room you built on the back of his house leaks like crazy."

Leaner wasn't alarmed. "Put Garcia on it, will you?" he said. "I'll square up with him when I get back to town."

Garcia was Leaner's ace in the hole. On impulse once, Leaner had placed Garcia in the trunk of his car during a raid by immigration authorities on his job site. As a result, Leaner could count on Garcia's fierce sense of loyalty as well as his expertise in construction work.

"What's his first name?"

"Juan, Juan Garcia. It's the Spanish equivalent of John Smith. His number's where I keep the paperwork. Lauren, I've got to run. Amelia's meeting me here and

I see her coming down the sidewalk. I'll call from the Catskills."

He put down the receiver firmly. It had seemed like a never-ending conversation. Suddenly Leaner remembered a dream he had had the previous night. Amelia had sung the kids a couple of songs accompanied by her dulcimer before putting them to bed, and Leaner could hear the sweet music drifting through the house. The dream must have been a carryover from that. In it, Amelia performed a dance around a fire, stripping off her clothes and throwing them into the flames. Leaner had to run to her with a blanket and wrap it around her. Damned strange. Pennsylvania was quite a state for stirring up the imagination.

"I found a telephone," Amelia said. "It's red. Now we're part of a society again."

He took the bag of food from her, and they walked to the car with the children. Leaner's concentration wavered. He wasn't seeing much of the scenery on the way to Amelia's house. Instead, he envisioned Lauren's backyard project. He could just see that stupid monkey leaping wildly from the dog's back, bull-dogging a runaway guinea pig in the grass.

6

APPREHENSION ABOUT THE impending golf tournament didn't allow Leaner much sleep during his last night at his sister's. He was wide awake well before sun-up. He dressed and slipped downstairs, sitting outside on the porch with a cup of coffee. Birds, silent as pine cones all night, were beginning to chirp in the morning's light. He wouldn't mind living here, but it would make going out for a movie or a pizza a bit difficult.

Amelia had moved onto the porch in utter silence, once again frightening Leaner by her abrupt presence.

"Can I join you?" she asked.

"Sure." They both sipped at their coffee, then he said, "Amelia, you ought to take up cigarettes."

"Why should I do that?"

"So you would be coughing in the mornings and someone could hear you coming and they wouldn't jump out of their skins because they thought they were all by themselves."

"I'll just tie some pots and pans to my feet for your next visit. How would that be?"

He didn't want an answer. Besides, it had now dawned on him that his time with his sister was drawing to a close. "I'm really glad I came to see you," he said.

"I feel badly that I didn't take you around more," she told him. "We never did go over to see Drake Well. They have a museum there, I understand."

"We'll make it next time," he said. "I'd like to see how those old oil derricks were put together. We did enough this time. We got to see that Amish community, or whatever they are. The trips into town were good. I like the area. It's peaceful, remote. The neighbors aren't breathing down your neck."

"It's more land than I'll ever need," Amelia said. "Why don't you clear a space on it and build yourself a house?"

"How cold does it get here in the winter?"

"About twenty below."

"That's pretty cold," Leaner said.

Then Leaner was packed, waving, and backing down the driveway before he knew it. He checked his atlas on the edge of the first paved road and mentally charted a route northward. He felt a certain urgency to cross over into New York as soon as possible, to get a slice of the Empire State under his belt before jumping right into the Catskills. So he veered through such Pennsylvania towns as Ormsby, Smethport, Coryville— fictional-sounding names from old James Stewart movies, solid little communities passing by, one by one.

Outside of Larabee, just shy of the New York state

line, he was slowed to about twenty miles per hour by a lumber truck struggling up the steep grades. Just when he thought he'd be able to pass it, the truck stopped in the middle of the road and let out a passenger. Leaner had no trouble recognizing him. It was Jonah, toting a canvas rucksack over his shoulder. Leaner cranked down a window and pulled up beside him.

"I'm going north, then east," Leaner said. "Do you need a ride?"

Jonah still hadn't gotten the hang of opening and closing car doors. He looked as if he were about to climb in the window once more, so Leaner threw open the door for him.

He drove a couple of miles before either of them spoke again. Jonah looked bewildered and rather tired.

"You're running away from home," Leaner said to break the ice.

"Yes," Jonah said. "That is my right."

"Is it that you're tired of living with your family, or you just don't like all the work? If you don't mind my asking."

"The work in the fields is good. For the body and the soul. I do not object to it." Jonah then shook his head, like a dog wringing the water from his scalp. "It is the *pinheads,*" he said. "I cannot bear another day with the pinheads."

"Look," Leaner said, "I know you're probably aggravated with your family, and you might have reason to be. But you shouldn't talk about them that way because they won't be around forever and you'll miss them when they're gone. Then how will you feel when you called them names? Do you see my point?"

"What?" Jonah didn't seem to make the connection. "Pinheads," Leaner reminded him. "Where did you learn such a word?"

"You misunderstand," Jonah told him. "Our community contains some two hundred people. We are all related. Some twenty-two of us, no, twenty-one now, are pinheads. My older brother is one."

"Not enough variety in the gene pool, huh?" Leaner said. "Listen, I didn't know. I apologize. It's just that I spent some time with my family for the first time in a while, and we were closer than I thought."

"We care for the pinheads in the large building you took me to. They cannot take care of themselves. It is something about their brains. A disease. The place is rather like a baby nursery."

Leaner tried to imagine them all together in one room, drooling on each other, playing patty-cake, hosed down in group baths. Something like an indoor penguin farm.

"There's nothing in my experience I can compare that to," he said.

"When you returned me home, I was made to care for the pinheads until early this morning. The punishment was fair. I have left on a new life. I owe them nothing."

"Good luck," Leaner said.

They crossed over into New York state, but the boundary was no panacea for Leaner's anxiety. A queasiness was hanging right in there. His palms began to sweat, and he developed a sudden headache. He knew what it was. He had been thinking about practically everything except the tournament for the past week, and now that he was in actual striking distance of the Catskills, it was Florida all over again. It was a classic case of stage fright mixed in with a good dose of bridal jitters. Leaner was grateful that he had not developed any discernible nervous tics. He couldn't stand seeing people with eye twitches, trapdoor blinks, jaw clamps, and bitten cheeks. Externally, he was a picture of composure.

"So what are your plans?" Leaner asked Jonah. "Going to the Big Apple and take on the town?"

"I am not certain of your meaning."

"Those are what you call slang terms. You'll be running into those from now on, so you'd better get used to them. I'm telling you this for your own good, you understand. I asked if you were going to New York City to look for a job."

"How far have we traveled?" Jonah asked.

"I don't know. Twenty, twenty-five miles."

"Would you believe me if I said to you that this is the greatest distance I have ever gone from home?"

Leaner glanced at the boy's homemade clothing and wondered what kind of tiny mind was at work under that silly starched yellow straw hat. "I believe it," he said.

"I have been educated at the farm. I know my numbers, and I am able to perform farm work of any kind."

"Well, that's in your favor," Leaner said, the conversation at least helping to settle his nerves some. "Of course, I don't know what the job market is like up here. But if a farmer needs to have his cows counted, I'd say you're in business." Amelia would have bawled him out for that smart-ass comment.

"I have money, but it would be better to find work before I had to spend it. Excuse me, but what is your name?"

"Thurmond Leaner."

"And what is your job, Mr. Leaner?"

"I'm a professional golfer," Leaner said, liking the sound of it.

Jonah winced and touched his fingertips to his forehead. "You mean to say," he said, "that you are given money to play the golf?"

"Breaking it down, I guess that's what I mean," Leaner said.

"Does a professional golfer...is it golfer?"

"It's golfer."

"Does a professional golfer have the need for an apprentice or a helper?"

"Now that you mention it," Leaner said, "I hadn't given it any thought, but I don't have a caddy. I was just going to hire one when the tournament started—"

Leaner felt a chill run up one arm, fantasized having a stroke or a heart attack, missing the tournament through ill health but attending it on a stretcher just the same, gaining a Jim Bowie kind of admiration from the galleries.

"Caddy," Jonah said, then repeated the addition to his vocabulary. "A caddy. Yes, I will be your caddy."

"You're hired," Leaner said.

"What will my duties be?"

"It's important that I don't get tired once play begins. It's your job to see that my clubs are handy when I need them. You just follow me wherever I go, and when I ask you for one, you give it to me. The clubs are numbered, so I'll just call out, say, 'Lemme have my six iron, Jonah,' and you'll hand over my six iron. That's about all there is to the job." Leaner wanted to stress to Jonah that although the job was simple, it was important. He didn't want to catch Jonah lollygagging around and interfering with the game's progress. Leaner set his jaw and talked out of the corner of his mouth. "You think you can handle that?"

"I can do it." Jonah even smiled.

"That sounds good," Leaner said. "I'll need you through next Sunday. The tournament is four days long. So I'll pay you for four days of work, plus a practice day. Five days. That's a work week in any man's factory, I'd say."

"Then we are working on the Sabbath?"

"Oh, yeah," Leaner said. "We have to. It's the final day. Of course, I might wash out after two days, and neither of us will have any work to do then. How does a hundred dollars sound?"

"That is agreeable," Jonah answered. It had taken him eighteen months to save the thirty-seven dollars in his rucksack.

"I'll just pull off the highway in one of these larger towns and cash a traveler's check," Leaner said. "And I can square up with you before we even reach the Catskills."

Although there was no rush to do so, Leaner exited at the first town they came to. He wanted to pay Jonah just in case he didn't remember to later. He had done that with Garcia a couple of times for subcontracting a job, and it proved to be embarrassing. Garcia was too shy and grateful to bring up the situation, and eventually Leaner would slap his forehead, perhaps while nailing shingles on a roof. "Jesus, Garcia," he would yell down, "let me get you that check."

"That's okay, Meester Leaner," Garcia would usually answer.

He found a bank but it was closed. Maybe small town banks shut down for lunch, but he doubted it. They drove around a few blocks and found another one that was in service. Leaner pulled in to the drive-in window, wrote a couple of checks and put them in the drawer. The clerk thanked him and in no time Leaner was stopped in the parking lot counting the money.

He gave Jonah the hundred, which the boy folded into a pocket, and suddenly they heard a strange noise, off in the distance and muffled by the buildings. Whatever it was, it gave the impression of a herd of elephants strangling in a pool of quicksand.

"I wonder what that could be," Leaner said.

He drove slowly around the block. The noise drifted in and out, and it was difficult to say from which direction it came.

"The people," Jonah said. "This is a town without people."

"I see what you're trying to say," Leaner said. "This is a regular mystery we have on our hands here, an Empire State mystery. We did see a bank cashier, so not everyone has disappeared. We really should get back on the road, but I've just got to find out what that noisy thing is."

They turned another corner. It was a parade, and it looked as if nearly the entire town was in it. Brightly uniformed marchers of every age were joined together doing unspeakable things to John Philip Sousa's "Stars and Stripes Forever." And the people in the small crowd lining the sidewalk all wore slightly puzzled, stoical expressions, a mixture of familial pride and sympathy.

Leaner wanted to get on out of there, but the parade encircled the block before he had a chance to escape.

Somehow his every exit was blocked, and the marchers were passing on all sides of his car. He didn't want to create a stir and drive right through them, but it did cross his mind. Each time he maneuvered the vehicle in a different direction, a section of the parade interfered.

Finally the flutists, of all people, came to his rescue, allowing a gap in front of them. Before they had a chance to close ranks Leaner stepped on the accelerator and went right through, Jonah hanging onto the door handle for dear life.

7

LEANER CHECKED INTO HIS
cabin on Monday evening, figuring that he would be
among the first of the golfers to arrive for the tournament, but when the desk clerk drew a line through his
name—indicating arrival, Leaner assumed—he noticed that were only two names remaining.

He walked outside the cabin after putting away his
luggage, Jonah trailing behind him.

"What am I to do?" he asked.

"I don't know," Leaner said. "There's not anything
for you to do until the practice round, so I guess you're
on your own until then." If you're lucky, he thought,
you might catch a rerun of "The Beverly Hillbillies"
on TV. It might help you feel a bit more at home. He
was improving. At least he didn't say it out loud.

Jonah decided he would go for a walk.

"Good idea," Leaner told him. "But watch out for
the natives. They may be armed."

Jonah paid no attention as he walked off. The boy
was learning fast, Leaner thought.

The cabins, it turned out, were situated adjacent to the golf course, arranged in rows like a little subdivision. Leaner saw one of his neighbors emptying a load of wine bottles and beer cans into a trash can.

"You Leaner?" the man asked when he saw him.

"That's right," Leaner said. "I just checked in."

"Cosmo Sherman," the neighbor said. "You say you just checked in. You mean into the cabin, or with Catalina?"

"No, I haven't met Mister Catalina yet," Leaner said.

"I've got a bottle inside. Could you use a drink?" Sherman said. "I need to talk, anyway."

"Sure," Leaner said, following him to the cabin next door.

Sherman poured bourbon into a couple of glasses, handed one to Leaner. "What do you know about Max Catalina?" he asked.

"Not too much. Only that he was among the top players in the thirties and used to pal around with Byron Nelson. That's about all I know about him. Why?"

"A year ago, that's all I knew." Sherman sighed, belted down the drink and poured himself another. "Did you read the fine print on your invitation or just sign it and send it back?"

"I just signed it," Leaner said. "I mean, what could be in it that would be contrary to regulation play?"

Sherman paced the room a couple of times, then nervously sat down. "It's not the play I'm worried about. Jesus Christ, if I was a half decent player I wouldn't be here except to rake a few bums. You know what Catalina had us do for a whole day last year? Horseshoes, for Christ's sake. You know what your backswing is like after eight hours of horseshoes? Now, Catalina may have been one of the best back in the Ice Ages, I'll grant you. But he's an old man now. He's *real* old. I think he may be getting senile. His idea of golf is to stage a tournament, invite every big name and every nobody in the business to play, and all he ends up with are the Cosmo Shermans and the Thurmond Leaners."

Leaner had never heard himself referred to in the plural, and was put off by it. It made him sound as if he were less than a whole person. But he could see that Sherman was worked up and figured he had better listen.

"What about the Lee Trevinos, the Jack Nicklauses?" Leaner wanted to know.

"They're wise to Catalina," Sherman said. "They can't stand him. You think Jack Nicklaus would spend a day pitching horseshoes? Of course not. And neither would I if any decent tournament—I don't mean the Master's, but a quality deal—felt like giving me a break, even half a chance to play." Sherman was into his third drink now. "I'll tell you, Thurmond, the man revels in humiliation. And that's just what it is, nothing less. It makes me damned mad."

"I can see that," Leaner said.

"Don't take my word for it. You'll see soon enough. Just don't make any plans for the next two days, because Catalina already has. We'll find out tonight in that nightclub of his when the opening foursomes are drawn up."

"What nightclub?"

"Oh, his damn clubhouse. It's huge."

Leaner returned to his own cabin and rummaged through his suitcase. He found his duplicate copy of the invitation and began poring over it. Sure enough, the document insisted that all players check in no later than Monday evening. Tuesday and Wednesday were reserved for "activities to be named at a later date." Monday evening was scheduled for dinner, entertainment and assigning the foursomes for the opening round. The entertainment was listed as a golf monologue by Bob Newhart. Leaner looked forward to that because Bob Newhart was one of his favorite living comedians.

A few minutes before eight Leaner left for the clubhouse, but stopped by Sherman's cabin on the way. Sherman had been drinking all afternoon, and even though there was no slurred speech or weave to his walk there was an edge about him that Leaner had to put on the liquor.

"I can't believe Catalina's springing for a dinner," Sherman said. "It'll probably show up on the cabin bill. He owns the cabins, you know."

"You're kidding."

"He owns the cabins, the clubhouse, the course, the works."

"He sounds well off," Leaner said.

"Catalina married into it when his game hit a slump. Some broad back in the late forties who owned a liquor store and bait camp on a private lake. That lake's a hazard on a couple of the holes now. The bastard's had a nice easy time of it."

"Aren't you a little hard on him?" Leaner asked. "You didn't have to come here."

"Answer that yourself in a week," Sherman said. "You'll see. I won't say I told you so. I'll just say you'll see. By the way, who *was* that I saw lurking around your cabin in that straw hat?"

"My caddy," Leaner said proudly.

"You got your own caddy? Jesus, what are you, one of Catalina's ringers?"

"What?"

"Catalina likes to sneak in a pro's pro. I suspect he splits the big shot's winnings with him, or is on the take somehow. There's not a damned thing you can do about it, though, other than beat him fair and square. This year the man to beat is Buck Hollingsworth."

"Hollingsworth is here?"

"You bet he is, with a hundred and seventy grand in winnings. Not bad for August."

"Well, he can't win every tournament," Leaner said.

"No, but a hundred and seventy grand. Jesus."

Leaner held the club door open for Sherman, and as they entered he said, "I can't wait to see Bob Newhart."

"Don't hold your breath," Sherman said.

They found a table near the stage. Sherman ordered a drink and checked out their fellow golfers. He recognized a few he'd played with before, nodding to them. Leaner searched the faces to see if he saw anyone from Florida, but as far as he knew none of those he had qualified with had made it to the Catalina Invitational.

"I still can't get over that Catalina is providing a meal for so many people. What do you want to bet that they bring out steam tables and it's a buffet of beans and franks?"

Leaner said, "I always kind of liked beans and franks."

"What the hell's the matter with you?" Sherman said, glaring at him. Leaner let it slide.

The house lights began to dim, and Leaner smiled in anticipation. But when the curtains parted the figure spotlighted on stage was not Bob Newhart. It was the desk clerk who had checked Leaner into his cabin.

"That's Leo Fenner." Sherman nudged Leaner. "Catalina's brother-in-law."

Fenner held a microphone and looked out into the darkened club, waiting for the patrons to settle down before speaking.

"Ladies and gentlemen," he began, and Leaner made a quick check of the room for ladies, saw there were a few. "Welcome to the twenty-third annual Max Catalina Invitational Golf Tournament, once again held here at the Catalina Country Club in beautiful Roscoe, New York. Max and I spoke about this year's field of players, and he agreed, or rather I agreed.... Well, he said it and I agreed that this is the best bunch of golfers to hit the Catskills in a decade." Scattered applause, but there were enough drunks in the audience to have applauded Fenner's nose. "Over the next week we hope to get to know you a lot better, and hope that you'll always remember that there's something even more important than winning. And that's being healthy enough to thank the good Lord above that there's such a game as golf, and we're all in the shape to play it, and play it well. You're the best in the world, you professional golfers, and we salute you. We wish each and every one of you the best of luck."

Sherman emptied a whole glass of booze.

"And now without further ado, I'd like to introduce a brilliant young comic making his first appearance in Roscoe. Let's hear it for *Joey* Fenner."

Sherman belted Leaner on the arm a couple of times. "There's your Bob Newhart. What did I tell you?"

There was a moan from the audience as Fenner the Younger took the microphone in hand and unbuttoned his formal tie in the fashion of Tom Jones. He tried to do both with the same hand, then rubbed the mike against the material of his shirt. It sounded like thunder.

"Thank you, ladies and gentlemen, thank you very much," Joey said. "I guess you can see, I'm not Bob Newhart. Uncle Max asked me to fill in at the last moment when Bob couldn't make it. Hey, and that's what it's all about. That's why we're here. Helping each other out."

"As long as you're in the family," Sherman said out of the side of his mouth to Leaner, at the same time grabbing onto his arm like a young Kid Doolin.

Joey was already sweating profusely. He wore glasses which began to ski down his nose, and his Adam's apple was yo-yoing from rapid swallowing.

"Uncle Max fixed me up in a room here," Joey began. "Boy, was it small. It was so little that when you made a fire in the fireplace—you know, if you got cold or felt like looking into a fire and you wanted to make one in the fireplace—well, you'd have to stand the logs on end because there wasn't enough room to lay the logs down sideways."

Dead silence.

"Thank you, ladies and gentlemen. Thank you very much. Say, did you hear the one about what you get when you cross a gorilla with a canary? And where it sits? I don't know what you call it, but when it lays an egg, it sits anywhere it wants." Joey was clearly disoriented. "Thank you, ladies and gentlemen, thank you very much. Please, take my wife..."

Moans from the crowd. Leaner wouldn't have been surprised to see Joey shoot himself right on stage. Or be shot.

"Say, speaking of my wife—no, wait. Thank you ladies and gentlemen, thank you very much. Say, speaking of my wife, she can be hell to live with. You know what she does if I don't let her have a little *amore* at least three times a week?"

At least he had delivered a straight line, Leaner thought. Now he was letting it sink in. But Joey waited too long, standing there pulling at his collar like Rodney Dangerfield but in reality gasping for breath.

"I'd tell you what she does, except she doesn't exist. I'm not married, I'm not even going with anybody. Thank you ladies and gentlemen, thank you very much."

That killed Joey's comeback, if such a thing had ever been possible. Amid shouts and insults, someone threw a drink. Joey looked at the crowd like a nauseous cow caught in a car's headlights. Leaner felt embarrassed for Joey. He wanted to tell Joey to toss it in, get the hell offstage and pack for a long trip.

Suddenly Joey fainted, or seemed to. It was his first and last laugh. The elder Fenner rushed to his side, managed to sit him upright with his head between his legs. Their backs were to the crowd, which was howling.

"There will be a short intermission," Fenner called from over his shoulder to the spectators.

"I'm getting a bad feeling about this whole thing,"

Sherman said. "I thought for a moment there that booze and my imagination might be running away with me, but Fenner and that Joey snapped me back to my senses."

"Maybe Bob Newhart just couldn't make it," Leaner tried.

"Newhart? You think Catalina ever contacted him? This whole tournament is low-rent. It's golf's skid row. In the same league with midget women's wrestling."

Leaner wasn't about to argue with him, but he was getting tired of his one-note song of horrors past and to come. "You remind me of my cousin Vernon," Leaner told him.

"What?"

"Nothing."

The meal turned out to be steak smothered with fresh mushrooms, baked potatoes, broccoli au gratin and a crisp green salad. "So I was wrong about the food," Sherman said.

The plates were cleared away, and Fenner the Elder was again spotlighted.

"Ladies and gentlemen, may I have your attention again? First off, I'm sure you share my concern for young Joey. He's all right, thank God. Just a little scared, and who wouldn't be?"

"I couldn't care less," Sherman mumbled at their table.

"But right now, let's get down to business. I have the rare honor..."

"Rare, my ass," from Sherman.

"...to introduce a man who needs no introduction."

"Then *skip* it," said Sherman.

"Max Catalina is more than a golfing legend."

"He's your bread and butter, Fenner."

"Here is a man who, at the height of his golf career, joined the armed forces of this great nation of ours."

"He was drafted."

"He was a tail-gunner in a B-17 in more than fifty missions over Germany."

"Tail-gunner on a fork lift in Trenton, New Jersey."

"But you know all this," Fenner went on.

"We know too much."

"Some of his golfing records are still unbroken."

"Because no one wants to play Death Valley buck-ass naked."

"What more can I say? Here's *Max Catalina!*"

The spotlight picked out Catalina in the audience and followed him to the stage. He was wearing an old-time golf outfit, the knickers and spats with baggy pleated pants, sleeve garters, and a cap on the side of his head.

"Look at him, just look at him," Sherman stage-whispered. "That hair kills me. Wait till you see his hair. It looks like it was transplanted from his asshole."

Leaner twisted around as Catalina passed.

"Thanks, Leo," Catalina said to Fenner. "By God, you're the backbone of this operation." Fenner could be seen waving off the compliment. "We're running a little behind," Catalina began, "so here's what we've devised as the opening foursomes. I've drawn up a chart of the hundred and twenty cabins you're all staying in. I'll pass out mimeos of the same chart so there'll be no confusion. We've arranged each foursome to be a cluster of four adjacent cabins, and they're listed in the order they'll tee off on Thursday morning. For example, the first group tees off at six-fifteen A.M. It consists of

Abe Fay, Joe Hatcher, Cosmo Sherman and Thurgood Leaper."

Leaner stiffened. He didn't want to interrupt Catalina, but he couldn't let the mispronunciation go until the tournament was over. He raised his hand.

"Yes?" Catalina said.

"That's Leaner. Thurmond *Leaner.*"

Catalina took his glasses, resting them on the end of his nose, studying his notes.

"We've got you down as Thurgood Leaper. But I'll change it if you say so."

"Thank you."

Suddenly Catalina looked put out. "All right, all right, let's move along. We get started on these distractions and we'll never finish. Okay, each cluster of cabins is a foursome. A pair of odd numbers, a pair of even ones. Now, each of those pairs will be partners in tomorrow morning's canoe races. See you bright and early at the lake."

Catalina stepped off the stage, bounding through the audience while chairs were pulled out and people started to leave. Sherman tapped Leaner on the shoulder. "Here we go again. Like I told you."

8

LEANER WAS COMFORTABLE IN his cabin, but he still wasn't sure whether he was going to have to pay for it or if it was part of the deal for playing in the Catalina Invitational.

He was glad to have a television and phone available, not that he had a constant need of either of them, but the change was welcome after the time he'd spent without them in his sister's tranquil Allegheny wilderness.

Jonah had slept on a couch and was no bother. Besides, with what he was paying him, there was a certain amount of guilt if he didn't throw a blanket on the couch for him.

In the morning, as Leaner dressed for the canoe races, Jonah asked if he could either watch or take part in the festivities. Leaner considered the festivities themselves so peculiar that he couldn't imagine a restriction on what kind of audience was allowed, so he said sure. "But if they say caddies can't be there, you'll have to come back to the cabin. You understand, don't you, Jonah? It might be a rule. And while I'm thinking about it, why don't you let me get you a new shirt? Those wool ones of yours could give you heat prostration."

"My own clothing is sufficient."

"A short-sleeved one might be better. Besides, you don't want to get laughed at."

Jonah rubbed the palm of one hand on the front of his shirt. He looked curious about something. "Mister Leaner," he said, "is it a custom for professional golfers to paddle canoes prior to playing the golf?"

"No, it isn't," Leaner said. "It seems to be one of those fine-print Catskill things you run into now and then."

Leaner hadn't seen Sherman moving around outside, and after unsuccessfully trying to reach him on the phone he sent Jonah over to his cabin. "He's my partner in the race," Leaner explained. "If I get disqualified because he doesn't show, they may not let me play in the tournament."

Sherman came out after Jonah had scarcely tapped on his door. He looked as if he had just finished soaking his head in a tub of water. His hair was slicked straight back and his eyes were covered with shades. His clothing had been slept in.

"Do me a favor, Leaner," he yelled from his porch steps, "keep that spook of yours and his summer wool out of my way. Now come on out and let's get this damned thing over with."

Leaner, who considered Jonah on the shy side, was surprised to see his caddy walk with him and Sherman three abreast. He was also glad to see him take Sherman's razzing in stride.

"Just where the hell are you from?" Sherman demanded. "You look like one of those Pennsylvania

Dutch to me. Am I right? What is it? Mennonite? Quaker? Amish? Squeamish?"

"Back off," Leaner said.

"He can't talk for himself?"

"If you upset my caddy you could hurt my game. I've had him along on every tournament since turning pro, so I'd just as soon you leave him be."

"Well, crap," Sherman said, "I didn't mean anything. Try to make a little morning conversation with a guy and he jumps all down your throat. Say, what kind of sports you got where you come from?"

"There is not much sport," Jonah said. "On some Saturdays, after the work is finished, we play whiffle."

"And what the hell is whiffle?"

"A person stands in a circle of other people and attempts to avoid being struck by the whiffle, which is thrown by someone in the circle. When he is struck, the person responsible takes his place in the circle. The whiffle is carved from wood. Women are not allowed to play."

"I guess not," Sherman said. "Whiffle bruises on women are a definite turn-off. Just don't mention that whiffle stuff to Catalina, because it sounds like his kind of entertainment. Damned near as entertaining as this canoe crap. I guess you know why professional athletes like myself and your boss here put up with this nonsense, don't you?"

Jonah shook his head.

"Because it's Catalina's style," he said. "He's a showman in the worst sense of the word, meaning he's the only audience he tries to please. Besides, it gives him a chance to see what we're made of."

"What are we made of?" Leaner said.

"Shit, my friend. Nothing but shit."

"Then at least we should float," Leaner said.

He was taking note of the course as they approached the lake. He wanted to get a feel for it and if possible play a practice round on it. He didn't want to tee up at the first hole Thursday morning cold and ignorant.

Jonah sat in the fairway near the lake while Leaner and Sherman joined the other golfers at the water's edge. Leaner introduced himself to a few of them and was walking around shaking hands when the group first caught sight of Catalina and Fenner.

They were barreling down the rim of the fairway in some kind of small convertible like an MG or Triumph. They slowed on their approach to the water, made a wide turn and took off again in the opposite direction. They were both smoking fat cigars.

"Those assholes," Sherman said.

Catalina, behind the wheel, turned the car around again and made for the lake, going faster and faster— and drove it, kerplunk, right into the water. Leaner was the first one in the lake. The only one, for that matter, except for Catalina and Fenner. He swam a few strokes toward the floating car, which changed directions in the water and came toward him. He didn't understand what was happening, and he stood in the waist-deep lake to find out.

It was, of course, an amphibious car, Catalina's latest toy. On closer inspection it wasn't much of a car, and it wasn't much of a boat, but it did have the ability to travel both on land and in water. Leaner stood in the lake as Catalina drove in a circle around him, the cigar tucked in a cheek beside a toothy grin. Golfers on the course applauded.

Leaner waded to the shore, where Sherman, shaking his head, reached out a hand for him. "And that, too, is Catalina's style."

"I guess I looked sort of foolish," Leaner said in understatement. "I'm going back to change clothes."

The phone began to ring just as Leaner entered his cabin.

"Hello."

"I ought to hang up on you."

"Lauren. I was in a hurry when I talked to you the other day. You sounded frantic and I just didn't have the time. I'm sorry."

"You have the time now?"

"Well, I'm all wet, and I have to be somewhere else right now, so I'm a little pressed. I guess I could talk while I change clothes."

"What happened?"

"I jumped into a water hazard after a car drove into it."

"Was anybody hurt?"

"No, just my feelings... You know, I really didn't bring enough clothes. Those were my good shoes I was wearing, too. I hope they don't warp when they dry."

"Thurmond, let's not talk about clothes. I'm not calling from Texas to talk about clothes."

"Right. Not when we can talk about monkeys."

She hung up on him.

Because of what he was doing—that is, undressing and putting on fresh clothes while he talked on the telephone—Leaner was in an awkward position, alternately balancing on one foot, sitting, switching hands for the phone and toweling dry. He hung up the receiver and shook his head. I don't have the time for that stuff now, he told himself. I'll play the tournament, concentrate on my game, then straighten out my life after Sunday.

By the time he returned to the lake it looked like all the players were there. Those who had not witnessed Leaner's dive into the lake had by now certainly heard of it. He felt conspicuous because of it, but was determined not to allow the incident to be blown all out of proportion. In other words, he decided to let it drop, and not go after Catalina in front of over a hundred witnesses.

As for Catalina, he was speaking now through a bullhorn from his amphibious position in the lake when Leaner rejoined Sherman.

"Have I missed anything?"

"Fenner had a little speech. It wasn't anything. Now Catalina's running over the rules of his race. I think he's making them up as he goes."

Fenner was at the controls of the boat now, steering the thing to keep Catalina facing the crowd while the engine idled.

"All right, men. Listen up," Catalina was saying. "We have only eight canoes, so each team is going to have to wait their turn. Believe me, nothing would please me more than to see the whole bunch of you out here at once. But we have to work with what we have, which is eight canoes."

"The man is out of his mind," Sherman said.

"It's only human nature to slack off when there's no incentive. I don't want to see you guys slacking off out here, and to make sure you don't, I've added some incentive. Leo here suggested a cash bonus for the fastest time, but I vetoed that. Since this is the largest field of players in the history of the Invitational, I decided we could get by with four fewer players. So, the pair with the slowest time today is getting cut from the tournament."

Rumblings in the assembled ranks.

"I know what you're thinking," the bullhorn amplified. "A team is two players, and I'm cutting four. There'll be two from today's competition and two from tomorrow's. And to be fair, today's two slowest teams will have a second trial against each other. That's something you don't get in life too often. A second chance."

"Can he do that?" Leaner asked.

"It doesn't sound legal," Sherman said. "But look at the odds. Four players gone from the whole field. That doesn't look too bad, and as they say, it *is* the only game in town."

"Who knows," Leaner said. "Buck Hollingsworth could be the one to get bumped. I'd sure rather not have to play him."

"You haven't caught on yet," Sherman said. "Hollingsworth is in on the take up to his elbows, probably as involved as Fenner."

"To the best of my knowledge," Leaner told him, "a golf tournament can't be fixed."

Sherman threw his hands up in the air. "I don't know why I bother with you. It's obvious you don't want to know the truth. And even after what happened at the lake. What's with you?"

Leaner didn't see that he needed to explain that this tournament, playing in it, believing in it, felt like life and death to him. He ran a hand through his hair, scanning the crowd for Jonah, then did a double take when he spotted him sitting cross-legged opposite an attractive woman in jeans and a wind-blown halter top. She had her hands on his hips.

"Well, well," Leaner said, and gestured.

Sherman looked up to see what he was talking about. "Looks like Whiffle has found a wool fetishist."

They watched her walk away with Jonah in the direction of the cabins.

"Attention men, attention," Catalina was announcing. "I want the first eight teams in their canoes. I'll be your starter and Leo's the timekeeper."

"Is that us?" Leaner asked.

"No, we're in the fifth race. Have you ever paddled a canoe?"

"No."

"Terrific. Neither have I."

The lake was a fairly large one, fifteen or twenty acres, and since it was a part of a golf course, the scenery had that artificial beauty Leaner associated with the carefully manicured lawns of the wealthy. But no one was thinking much about scenery. The golfers were in a position to be disqualified for something that had nothing whatsoever to do with their ability at golf. They were to row from one extreme of the lake to some buoys, reverse their direction and return to their starting point.

None of this, of course, was sanctioned by the PGA. Catalina's was a renegade tournament, and he had the finances to privately sponsor the event year after year. The Catalina Invitational paid nearly as well as any on the pro circuit. It just didn't count for much in furthering one's golf career. Right now, as Leaner stood with arms crossed and stared into the glare on the water, watching grown men acting like fools for their survival, he kept an eye on the patron of the affair. Max Catalina was out there in the water among the eight canoes, his brother-in-law Fenner at the boat's controls while he barked commands and egged the golfers on through his bullhorn. "Put your backs into it, boys," Leaner could hear drifting across the lake. "Get the lead out, Ferguson. Raise a little sweat...."

The canoes were going in every direction. Few if any of the golfers had much experience in canoes. The eight would start out parallel and pointed in the same direction, but halfway across the lake they were strewn all over the water. It was agony for some of them. Most of the year the majority of them worked in other professions and let themselves get out of shape. The Catalina was the only tournament many of them could play in. After a race there were always two or three nearly heaving after beaching themselves on a nearby green, hunched over, hands on their knees.

The golfers outnumbered the spectators at this point. During the first four races the only half-hearted cheering came from a gang of boys who had shown up. It was summer, and if the kids were anything like Leaner had been when he was a boy, they stayed outside, showing up at home only for meals, baths and sleeping. Leaner wondered, though, why an elderly pipe-smoking man was there. "I'm retired," the man said when he asked. "There's not much else to do around here."

Now it was time for Leaner and Sherman to board their canoe from a rickety little pier. Leaner got in first, holding onto the pier as Sherman tentatively followed. The thing rocked violently and nearly went over.

"Sherman, get in the center, and farther up front."

"Here we are, folks," Sherman addressed an imaginary multitude. "Roscoe, New York. The big time. The Catalina Invitational. Doesn't it make you want to throw up?"

They had almost no time to practice their balance before Catalina fired his starting pistol, but their canoe racing form appeared to be no worse than their competitors'.

Leaner was in the rear of the canoe. He just happened to have gotten in that way, and thought how Catalina allowed a good half-hour between races. Trying to figure it out, he decided that Catalina just didn't want the festivities to end at noon. Sherman thought differently. "He's giving the bookies time to get their bets down."

They had lined up with the others, with Catalina a few yards ahead, and bang they were off, splashing, paddling and cursing. Leaner hoped and prayed that Sherman would not play the clown, that after driving all the way to the Catskills, those sorry damned back-east hills, his partner wouldn't get a wild hair up his ass and play human torpedo on the other canoes. Leaner's arms ached. Paddling was an abnormal exercise, as unnatural as a golf swing, and now an old man, out of reach by a few paddle lengths, was harassing them all. "You bums," he was shouting. God, he's right, Leaner was thinking. We are bums. The canoe won't go straight. We're not to the middle of the racecourse yet, and some of the others are already meeting us head on. We're losing. "Row harder, Sherman. Goddamn it, I'm not going back to Texas looking for more work. Beat me on the course, I won't care, but this is crazy."

They were approaching the anchored buoys. "Sherman, when we get there we don't have time to circle it and come back. We're way behind, so *listen*. At the buoy turn around in your seat and face me. Then I'll turn around and we'll take off again. You got it?"

Sherman nodded. He was terribly hungover.

As poorly as they rowed, the maneuver saved them nearly a full minute. Leaner felt like he was going mad. The others were out of the water. Leaner and Sherman were dead last as they hit the bank at the finish line and piled out onto the shore.

They finished fourth from the bottom out of all sixty pairs. But so far, they had qualified to play in the tournament.

"I don't see that damn Buck Hollingsworth anywhere," Leaner panted.

9

IT WASN'T THAT LEANER
enjoyed being taken advantage of. He was just a touch
slow to realize when it was happening. But when it
dawned on him that he was putting more into a situation than he was drawing in return, he got frustrated,
and angry. Like now. He needed to do something to
even up the scales.

After the canoe race he didn't hang around for an
extra minute. As soon as he caught his breath he was
stomping back to his cabin, still hearing Catalina jumping all over the present contestants on the lake. Leaner
was thinking about marching up the steps to his cabin,
kicking in the door and trashing the place. Maybe let
the bathtub overflow, or hide sandwich meats in obscure places to foul up the air after he'd left.

He wasn't far from the cabins when he remembered
Jonah and the girl. What if they were occupying Leaner's
bed, creating a hardy Catskill/Allegheny-Dutch stain
on the sheets? Leaner would kick his ass out, hundred
dollars or no hundred dollars. Just because Jonah had

endured a lot from pinhead relatives was no reason to sympathize with his running amok in the cabin. He felt protective of Jonah, but at the same time he was having second thoughts about having a roommate.

Leaner turned down an alley toward his cabin and was ashamed for what he'd been thinking when he saw Jonah washing his car. He hadn't asked him to do it.

"You're washing my car," Leaner said with no particular emphasis on any word.

Jonah dropped his sponge into the bucket. "You have a visitor," he said. "She awaits inside."

Leaner scrubbed the door-kicking impulse and entered quietly. Sitting on the couch holding an unlit cigarette was the woman Jonah had last been seen with. She looked at Leaner with a certain show of recognition. He wondered if he was supposed to know her from somewhere.

"Hello, I'm Thurmond Leaner."

"I know," she said. "I saw you at the lake."

"I see," Leaner said, hoping for an explanation.

"Aren't you curious?" she said.

"How do you mean that?"

She stood up, pulled off her top and started working on her pants. The front door wasn't even closed. It was all fairly arousing for Leaner, but he hesitated.

"Wait a minute," he said. "This may sound old-fashioned, but I have someone at home, and I've never been unfaithful. It's nothing to do with you. It's just the way I am. Will you leave?"

With that, Leaner locked himself in the bathroom

and took a hot shower. He had just done the sort of thing the motive for which he couldn't exactly put his finger on. Fidelity was something that was fairly ingrained in him, but while he stood there in the shower, he became more relaxed, and recalled the phone call from Lauren earlier in the day, and thought about how everything was pretty much a shambles right now. And he remembered his promise to himself to straighten things out after the tournament, which he now rationalized into a little behavioral leeway. So, he had passed this one up. He could have gotten laid, but now he was taking a shower instead. Who knew about the next time?

He walked out with a towel wrapped around him. She was still there, lying on the bed without a stitch on. Without hesitation he let the towel fly, and moved on top of her.

On a strictly impersonal, physical level it was wonderful, a fantasy played out. Leaner hadn't been with another woman in nearly two years. Ever since teaming up with Lauren, he had had no reason to stray. Some of their sessions in bed were better than others and, all told, he was satisfied with her, and she with him. But making love with this stranger was another kettle of fish altogether. She was quite vocal, for one thing, and if Lauren made an occasional whimper or animal noise, this woman sounded like the forest fire scene from *Bambi*. She just went on and on with the sounds: moans, cries, and a shriek here and there. And Leaner rode her out until the animals all ran away. Lying on his side, he happened to glance out the window. He couldn't believe what he saw. Jonah was pressed against the glass, and there was no telling how long he'd been there.

"That little sneak has been watching us," Leaner said.

"I know. I was getting off on it. You know, screwing and being watched. I pretended he was my husband and you were my brother. My name's Margot. I like fantasies."

"Nice to meet you, Margot," Leaner said as Jonah disappeared. "What I told you earlier was true. I've never been unfaithful until now. Don't misunderstand. You were tremendous a minute ago. It's just that I'm feeling kind of rotten inside. I guess it's guilt."

"I could leave," Margot suggested.

"Would you do that?" Leaner said with relief. "I think I'd be better off alone for a little while to kind of figure out what's going on with me."

"Sure," she said.

She dressed and let the screen door slam behind her. Leaner put on his clothes, then stretched out again in bed. "I did tell her no first," he said aloud. "That's more than a lot of guys would have done."

But Leaner knew that his resistance had been a token one. If Margot had not been waiting for him to finish showering, he probably would have sought her out. There weren't that many hiding places at Catalina's, and he pictured himself tracking her down on the course in a golf cart.

But was this really guilt he felt, or was it a carryover from his walk from the lake to the cabin? Running into Margot should have balanced the scales again, or even tipped them in his favor. And it was true that the canoe race didn't occupy his thoughts now. So he concluded that it was, indeed, guilt. "I can see my gravestone now," he said. "'Here lies Thurmond Leaner, Minor Golfer and Fornicator.'"

He fell asleep and napped the rest of the afternoon.

10

IT WAS ONE OF
those heavy, dreamless sleeps that leaves you clammy,
the kind that takes two cups of coffee to wake up from,
and you still think a day has passed but it's only late
evening.

Leaner wanted to have a talk with Jonah to point out
a few of the do's and don't's about how to behave away
from the farm. Some people might not think anything
of being spied upon while in the sack. Margot certainly
didn't. If anything, it enhanced the experience for her.
But Leaner wasn't like that, and he was determined to
set Jonah straight in that area. Voyeurism was inex-
cusable in Leaner's eyes, at least when it involved himself.

At about ten he went looking for Jonah at Sherman's
cabin.

"He was here earlier," Sherman said, feet propped
beside the portable TV. "I fixed him two drinks. He
went to the bathroom and got sick. Blew beets for
twenty minutes. The same thing happened to me the

109

first time I got drunk. I had to ask him to leave, because he started missing the toilet, and I had to get in there to take a leak."

"All right, all right," Leaner said. "I just asked if you'd seen him. I really don't care what's been going on in your bathroom."

"You don't need him tomorrow, anyway," Sherman said. "We'll be spending the day playing Scrabble. That was the announcement after you left early from the lake. Two players to a team, best five games out of eight. The two lowest scores are eliminated from the tournament."

"I would have thought it would be more strenuous than Scrabble. But you know what I'd really like right now? Some ribs. Barbecued ribs."

"Forget about ribs," Sherman said. "There's a grocery open down the road, and that's about it. If you're going, let me come with you."

On the way out of Catalina's compound Leaner's headlights caught Jonah bent over on the side of the road. He looked pale and shaken. Leaner braked the car and rolled down his window. "Don't peek in windows," he said, taking off again.

"What was that about?" Sherman asked.

"Personal business," Leaner said.

"Sounds to me like someone's about to get assigned to the caddies' barracks."

"I didn't know there was a place for caddies," Leaner said. "That makes things easier. Out he goes in the morning."

"Hey, Leaner, answer me a question." Sherman said it like he had something really important on his mind, like what to do with Northern Ireland, or should the electoral college be dismantled.

"If I can," Leaner said.

"How come you didn't want to eat at the club?"

"I guess I wanted off Catalina's property for a while."

"There you go," Sherman laughed. "The man deserves any ill will and all the resentment we can muster. You're finally coming around."

"Mostly I just needed out of the cabin."

In the store, Leaner decided that he might as well go ahead and buy some provisions for the duration of the tournament. There was a kitchenette in the cabin with a little waist-high refrigerator, a two-burner stove and the smallest sink east of New Orleans. Leaner had seen cantaloupes that wouldn't fit in the sink. About all that Leaner could buy in the store without placing a special order to Albany was a loaf of white bread, packs of ham and turkey skins, and a family-size bag of potato chips. It was as if the store maintained the town on a diet of sandwiches.

"We have cheese, too," the cashier pointed out to Leaner.

"Maybe next time," he said as he paid up.

Leaner threw the stuff into the back seat and sat behind the wheel. He still wanted ribs.

"That'll set you up for a few days," Sherman said.

"That's how I look at it," Leaner said. "I'll be out of here soon."

"Could be sooner than you think."

"The Scrabble?" Leaner said. "I'm not too worried."

Sherman watched the scenery in the headlights, cleaning his front teeth with his tongue as if something

were caught in there. "You know a girl named Margot?"
he said.

Leaner tensed up. "Why?" he said, louder than he'd
planned.

"Seems to me," Sherman said, really digging with
the tongue now, clucking and pausing for effect, "seems
if a fellow wanted to make an impression on Max Catalina, all he'd have to do is, say, get caught humping
Margot Catalina in broad daylight with the front door
of his cabin wide open."

"Margot *Catalina*?" Leaner said. "I had no idea." He
could feel his pulse in the heat of his face. He swal-
lowed. "Wife or daughter?" he asked.

"Granddaughter," Sherman said. "She's nineteen.
She's spending the summer with her grandpa."

Considering the possibilities, he felt almost relieved.
He knew perhaps there was something to panic about,
yet he relaxed his grip on the steering wheel and felt
his back ease against the seat.

"You saw her with Jonah," he said. "Why didn't you
say something then?"

"Without my glasses she could have been Eleanor
Roosevelt. I found out and I've given you a word to the
wise, that's all. Keep it in mind tomorrow while we're
playing Catalina and Fenner in the Scrabble tournament. Someone had to take the place of the two guys
who got eliminated in the canoe race, and guess who
volunteered?"

"Bring 'em on," Leaner said. "I figure I can handle a
couple of old toads like that."

"What if those old toads spend a week each year at
this tournament, and the other fifty-one weeks a year
playing Scrabble?"

* * *

Because of his afternoon nap Leaner was awake nearly all night. He finally dropped off to sleep around four. When he awoke in the morning it was to the sound of Jonah finishing off the bag of potato chips. Leaner cut loose.

"Get out," he exploded from the bed. "Pack your bag and get out of here. I don't want to see you until five-thirty tomorrow morning when we tee off."

Jonah was ashamed. It was his first exposure to junk food, and he really couldn't stop himself once he began eating the chips. He went through the whole bag, even to the point of crackling the paper to make the corners cough up the few final crumbs. He was still holding the bag as Leaner berated him.

"And don't look so damn *forlorn*," Leaner said. He was rolling now. It had been ages since he'd used the word "forlorn," but there it was waiting for him just when it fit right in. "You can quit now and be done with it. If that's your decision, hand over your wages and thumb your ass back to those Keystone pinheads. If you do stay, ask around where the caddies bunk and please keep out of my sight for the rest of the day."

Leaner had never taken a course in public speaking. If he had, he would have learned the importance of his posture. Credibility diminished the longer one lay prone facing the ceiling. But Jonah hadn't heard that many speeches before anyway, so he was as impressed as Moses listening to the words from the burning bush.

"I would like another chance, sir," he said.

Leaner pulled a pillow over his head until he heard Jonah leave. He tried to get back to sleep but was awake for the day. He could tell. At least he had Jonah out of the way. The pecking episode had set up, and the potato chips had clinched, his banishment to the caddies' barracks. But if neither had happened, Leaner would have invited him out anyway.

"I might as well get on up," he said aloud.

Once he threw on some clothes he felt almost giddy, unaware that his mood was riding a roller coaster lately. He bounded over to Sherman's cabin, elated now to have him as a partner. Sherman seemed to know all the ropes, and it helped to have an experienced guide in the Catskills. Leaner found him taking a slug from a flask. "Just one minute," Sherman said. "Got to brush my teeth."

"Then what?"

"Then it's off to the club. The tables have been set up with Scrabble boards. Have you considered why Catalina has a foursome playing itself in Scrabble?"

"I hadn't given it much thought."

"I have," Sherman said, squeezing toothpaste onto his brush. "He wants us to get mad at each other, so the very guys you have to play on the field have all these grudges already built up, if not from the canoe race then from the sneaky stuff in the Scrabble."

"But we're playing Catalina and Fenner. You said so."

"Don't I know it," Sherman said bitterly, spitting out a mouthful of suds. "They're up to something," he said, pointing the brush at Leaner in the mirror. "And I'm not taking any more crud from the likes of the Catalina clan."

"Loosen up," Leaner said. "Easy. We're partners, after all."

*   *   *

Leaner and Sherman made their way inside. It was very confusing. The tables were set up with placards naming who was to be sitting where, and people were wandering around all over the place reading the lists. In contrast to yesterday's event no one was doing much in the way of mingling. Generally, they just wanted to get the silliness out of the way and shoot some golf.

"Look, there's Fenner," Leaner said. "I'll ask him where our seats are."

Sherman kicked one leg out to the side, and brought it back slowly, squeezing out a high-pitched fart. "All right."

Fenner was all smiles when Leaner approached him. He was holding something under his arm that looked like a stack of menus. Leaner introduced himself, explaining that he and Sherman were squared off with the Catalina-Fenner team. "Ah, yes. Come this way," Fenner said, taking off like an usher in a crowded church, sideways through the crowd like a sand crab, holding whatever it was he had high above his head. Leaner stayed close behind him, almost feeling he should break into a samba to snake his way through all the people.

"Make room, make room," Leaner could hear Fenner saying.

The table was empty. Once Leaner was seated and Fenner made himself scarce again, Sherman appeared. "Have you seen Catalina?"

"Not yet," Leaner said. "But I haven't really been looking for him."

"I hate this," Sherman said. "I really hate this."

"It won't be long now, anyway," Leaner said.

"If that's supposed to be comforting, it fell a little

short," Sherman said as he sat down. "It won't be long now. That was probably said dozens of times by the passengers of the *Titanic* as the water closed over their heads." Sherman shook his head slowly, looking up and down the rows of tables. "Here he comes, patting guys on the back as he goes. God, I can't stand it. He's getting closer. When he gets to our table I'm going to *hit* him. Do you hear me? I'm going to *hit* him."

Leaner didn't know what to do. Sherman looked all worked up. He might really do it.

"Don't be an idiot, Sherman. You'll get run out of town, not to mention the tournament." He looked over his shoulder. Catalina had stopped to talk with someone. He was laughing.

"I *told* you I wasn't taking any more of his crud," Sherman said. "When he gets to the table I'm going to stand up and knock him cold. He'll never know what happened until he reads it in the paper."

Catalina was ten steps away, now five. He stood at the table and pulled out a chair. Sherman got to his feet, and Leaner closed his eyes, squinting like a dog being hit with a rolled-up newspaper.

"Mister Catalina," Leaner heard Sherman say, "you don't know how Thurmond and I have been looking forward to this. Really, you don't."

Leaner opened his eyes. Sherman and Catalina were shaking hands. Sherman slipped Leaner a wink. Catalina extended his hand to Leaner. "I've heard some good things about you," he said. Leaner smiled and nodded, thinking the statement was frankly impossible. At about the moment he was stepping into the canoe he had decided that his invitation to the tournament had been a fluke, like landing on a junk mail list. Only chance had brought him here.

"Thank you," Leaner said.

"Is this your first visit to the Catskills?"

"Yes, it is."

"I hope you enjoy your stay here."

"I have so far."

They all sat down, Leaner and Sherman opposite each other, Catalina between them, facing rigidly forward. When Catalina spoke, his eyes shifted from one of them to the other, but his head never moved. This tended to be unnerving to those he sat with.

"You don't know what a pleasure this is for me," Catalina said. "To attract you players from all across this country of ours. We even have a player from Hawaii this year, a Mr. Toshiba. I swear, if I could do it year round, I would. Once a year, it seems to be here and gone before you know it. Like Christmas, I guess. I like to make it last as long as possible. That's one reason I include two days of nongolfing activities in the Invitational. And the players. You boys form a camaraderie that's hard to believe. If it's selfish of me to want to see you boys having such a good time, then by gum, I'm a selfish old man."

"Oh, it's been *great* fun," Sherman said. "I never dreamed that rowing a goddam canoe could get you almost as sore as eight hours of horseshoes."

"Then you were here last year." Catalina smiled. "It may not be modest of me to say so, but most of the players come back year after year. Ray Reasoner has played in twenty straight. He holds the record. He's back this year, too. Say, those horseshoes were fun, weren't they? The doctor won't let me do things like that any more. That's the trouble when you get older. You slow down, you have less energy. But golf keeps me young. I wouldn't have lived this long without golf. Wouldn't have wanted to."

"And how long is that?" Sherman asked. "Ninety? Ninety-five?"

Catalina chuckled. "I wish Leo would get moving. We're running late again."

Fenner was distributing the score sheets Catalina had printed up especially for the occasion. They were what he'd been carrying when he seated Leaner. When Fenner passed the table, Leaner took a sheet and examined it. Instead of just a plain piece of paper, one side of it listed all kinds of trivia about Catalina's career and his tournament. Leaner looked down the list of past winners. He had heard of only one, and that was because his name had just been brought up—Ray Reasoner, first place, 1974.

Leaner found it easier to get wrapped up in the Scrabble score sheet than to follow the conversation. Sherman was being pretty ugly right to Catalina's face, and it was difficult to tell if Catalina really was aware of what was being said to him. He seemed to hear only what he wanted. Leaner didn't know whether Catalina was hard of hearing or senile. Probably, he thought, a little of each.

Next, Fenner passed out the Scrabble games themselves. He had help from his boy Joey, the comedian manqué. Fenner joined them at the table as soon as he could.

"What took so long, Leo?" Catalina asked. "We've been waiting for you."

Fenner wiped his brow, even though he wasn't sweating.

"Things take time," he said. "Nobody knew where to sit. There were a lot of boards to handle, fifty-nine to be exact. We can start now."

Catalina took that as his signal to rise from his chair and shout to the golfers, "Gentlemen, let's play Scrabble." He then sank into his chair and faced straight ahead again.

They drew their letters. Leaner's play was to open the game. It had been years since he played Scrabble, and he couldn't remember ever being too fond of it. In his first draw he had only two consonants and could envision no blitzkrieg attack on his opponents with what he had. Fenner started drumming the table with his fingers, and Leaner was anxious to lay something down to get the game rolling. To speed things up he settled on a nondescript four-letter word, yielding few points for his side.

Then Catalina, Sherman and Fenner played in quick succession, and it was Leaner's turn again. No one had spoken since the game had begun, not even at the other tables. It gave the room the impression of a college final exam. Leaner studied his letters, wondering if talking was allowed during play. Perhaps an obscure Catskill rule could be invoked, a rule where whoever said anything had the total of his spoken words deducted from his team's score.

He risked an early setback by blurting out, "I sure have some lousy letters," half-expecting Catalina to clap his hands together joyously, and rapidly tally up Leaner's penalty.

"I know what you mean," Fenner said.

Murmurs could be heard now from all over the club. Things were beginning to be more casual. Leaner decided he had spent enough time. He hardly had a play, and his choice of letters was so limited that he thought he would be forced to spell CAT. He thought that might be a reflection of ignorance, and at the last second substituted a P for the T.

"Cap," Leaner said. "C-A-P."

"Seven points," Catalina said. "My turn." Catalina logged the score. His fingers moved from the pencil to his letters. He deftly rearranged their sequence time after time. He looked like someone who could deal cards well. Catalina looked up from his letters, to Sherman and then to Leaner.

"I'm afraid I have you," he said. " 'Capricious.' Triple word, that's forty-eight, plus fifty for using all my letters. Ninety-eight." He reached for the pencil and added the score.

"Nice going, Leaner," Sherman said. "Talk about a setup. What the hell were you thinking?"

"What are you saying?"

"I had good letters," Catalina said to Sherman. "It wasn't your partner's fault."

Sherman shut up. The first game was catastrophic for him and Leaner. They averaged some eleven points per play to their opponents' twenty-eight. Nearly every triple word play went to Catalina or Fenner, as did the majority of the double words and bonus letters. But Sherman had sneaked in the Q and the Z, and since a total of five games were under consideration, any given game didn't necessarily have the importance of a one-play sudden-death match.

The second and third games were like the first. There

was little doubt that Fenner and Catalina were Scrabble wizards. Ringers, actually. But Leaner-Sherman were improving if still losing. Catalina assured them all was well. "You're getting good letters," he said. By the end of the third game they were averaging a little over nineteen points per play.

By this time it appeared that Sherman's assessment of the Scrabble competition was on target. Several arguments had broken out in various sections of the club. Usually the agitation was settled by a closer examination of the rules. One could look across the room and see that the underside of the game's lid was under reference nearly constantly. One disagreement, however, nearly came to blows, and one golfer-scrabbler had to be physically restrained as he shouted, red-faced and jugular, "You can't pull a hyphen on me and get away with it, you son of a bitch."

A play Sherman made in the fourth game tied the score for the first time. It wasn't so much that they were playing great as that their opponents were getting a poor draw.

"I have four I's," Fenner said, disgusted with the turn of events.

"The game's not over yet, Leo," Catalina was quick to point out. "There are still some good letters out there."

It was Leaner's play when he happened to see Margot coming toward the table. Offhand, he couldn't think of anyone else who had the potential for stirring a little pandemonium into so sedate an activity as Scrabble. Leaner became stalled at the board. He envisioned her doing any number of things. Point him out to her grandfather, stuttering, "He's the one who-who-who ... *raped* me." Or simply hop onto the table, kicking away the game along with most of her clothes before stripping off the rest of her attire.

She stood between Leaner and Catalina now, wearing a dark blue skirt with a little white top that looked like a sailor's outfit, and she had a nice subtle fragrance about her. Leaner breathed in slowly, not choosing to look her in the face. Was it sandalwood? "Who's winning, Granddaddy?" she asked.

"It's close," Catalina told her.

Margot sat in her grandfather's lap and gave him a couple of kisses on the cheek.

"That's my little honey pie," Catalina said.

Leaner was so distracted that he practically threw a pair of letters onto the board and let them land where they might. It was an eight-point effort. Margot wrapped her arms around Catalina's neck and watched the play progress. She lay her head on his shoulder, and when Leaner happened to look up, she rubbed his leg under the table.

Leaner stood up. "What do you say we take a break?"

Catalina never looked away from his letters. "We don't take breaks."

Margot gave Leaner a pout, thrusting out her lower lip and sighing a time or two.

"Driving me nuts," Leaner said, taking his seat again.

"What's that?" Catalina said.

"You're driving him nuts," Sherman said. "You're driving us all nuts."

Catalina squeezed Margot. "What did they say, honey pie?"

"Nothing, Granddaddy."

Catalina tried turning an M upside down to pass it

off as a W, but Margot slapped his hands. "No, Grand-daddy. That's against the rules."

Hours passed. Leaner was weak from hunger, and his seat ached as if he'd driven from Texas in one day. He was sure that Catalina's legs had to be asleep by now, with Margot sitting all the time in his lap. She had worked her shoes off and was rubbing Leaner's crotch beneath the table, right in front of her grandfather. Leaner couldn't believe she could be so bold, and he was certain Fenner was aware of what was going on.

Catalina just went on with his play, smiling.

Back in his cabin, Leaner was irritated with himself for not getting there sooner to check out the course, so he wolfed down a turkey sandwich and headed for the pro shop to rent a golf cart. If there wasn't enough daylight left to shoot a practice round, at least he could take a good look at the course. When he arrived at the shop he found there were no carts, and so he would have to step off as much of the course as possible until it got too dark.

He was squatting on the third green, examining the break and the grain, when Margot pulled up in Catalina's little car-boat. She braked on the cart path and walked up right behind him.

"What are you doing?"

"Seeing how the greens break. There's not much time left."

"How do you like my underwear?"

Leaner turned around. Margot had hiked her skirt up. She wasn't wearing anything under there.

"That's very cute and amusing, Margot," he said, "but I have my livelihood to consider right now, so why don't you just beat it and go warm your grand-daddy's lap."

"You don't know the shivers I get from cruelty."

Leaner suddenly grabbed her by the hair, forcing his mouth against hers, biting her lip. He broke the connection as abruptly as he had made it, and she fell on her back into the sand trap. Margot mistook his behavior for an erotic frenzy brought on by her talk of cruelty. Leaner was just calling her bluff... he was also annoyed.

Margot raised herself on her elbows, still on her back. Leaner put his hands on his hips in a King-and-I sort of pose. She ran a hand through her hair and pouted.

"You're my *man*."

"Why didn't you tell me you were Catalina's grand-daughter?"

She spoke to the sand. "I wanted you to want me for what I am, not who I am."

"What are you?"

"I have to tell my man I'm his willing slave?"

"Leaner jumped down into the sand and helped her up. "Look," he said, "I told you before I'm somebody else's man. If you want to do me a favor, drive me to the next green. But no more of this slave business. Will you promise me that?"

Her answer was to drive like a mad person, the wind blowing her hair, her skirt hiked up to her crotch. Leaner told himself not to look—an instruction he, of course, paid no attention to.

11

LEANER WOULD NOT HAVE
believed a week earlier that he would ever play golf at
such an hour. It was still completely dark outside as
he sat on the edge of the bed. Even the birds had the
good sense to wait for daylight before commencing their
day's activities. Catalina couldn't surprise Leaner now.
A pre-dawn round of golf went with the Scrabblefest.

He pulled on some pants with the bedside lamp on
low. At some time during the night they had woken
up freezing to death, and one thing led to another, and
there was quite a bit of horsing around.

He put on socks and a shirt, sitting down beside her.
Leaner wondered how old Margot was. He was never
good at judging someone's age, the range from eighteen
to thirty being particularly nebulous for him. Once in
high school Leaner had picked up his blind date,
whisking her from her porch to a baseball game in the
Astrodome. They were having a great time; they necked
a little in the parking lot, and once inside the dome
were laughing at everything, anything. During the

seventh-inning stretch Leaner's date confessed that she was thirty-five, twice his age. "Barbara's my daughter, she was still getting ready when you drove up and before I had a chance to say anything we were in your car. What the hell, my daughter'll kill me, but you looked cute, and frankly I could use a little action with a young'un." Leaner had done his best to oblige.

Margot stirred now while Leaner put on his golf shoes. She opened her eyes and looked at him sleepily but a bit smugly.

"How old are you?" Leaner asked.

"Twenty."

"You don't look it."

"Don't leave me," she said.

"It's time. I can just make breakfast in the club before I tee off."

"Eat real fast," Margot said, drawing the sheet over her breasts. "Then lie down here with me before you leave."

"I really have to go—"

"Aren't you in love with me yet?"

"Margot, we haven't even brushed our teeth together yet."

She embraced him, working his shirt open and planting kisses around his neck and shoulders. Her hand went exploring inside his pants.

Leaner took hold of both her wrists and pressed them onto the bed. "Not now," he said. "It's time to play golf."

"Well, what the hell am I supposed to do all day?"

"I don't know," he said, standing up. "You'll think of something."

"I can't believe my man's not in love with me yet,"

she said. "And he's speaking ever so hatefully."
Leaner picked up his clubs and walked out.

"Catalina's granddaughter couldn't be any stranger,"
Leaner told Sherman in the club over breakfast.
"What's the problem?" Sherman asked. "She doesn't
know you're just screwing her while you're here, then
you'll drop her when it's time to leave?"
   "Did you have to put it that way?" Leaner said. "I'm
not feeling so hot, without hearing that. Lauren's in
Houston looking for a saddle for our dog so a monkey
she bought can ride it and make her some money. Catalina's torturing us, and Margot keeps saying things I
wish she wouldn't... God, I feel like we're about to go
duck hunting. Is it even light outside yet?"
   "I don't know," Sherman said. "I guess we should
wait for Catalina. He's supposed to come to the club
before we tee off."
   "I'm not playing until I can *see*," Leaner said.
   Sherman finished his coffee. "Ordinarily, that's a good
plan, but don't forget where we are. When Mister Catalina says the tournament begins, it begins. He's going
to make up our foursome with Ray Reasoner."
   "Oh, no."
   "Yes, it's a symbolic and sentimental gesture of his
that's become quite a tradition in the Catskills."
   "Maybe he'll just play a hole or two," Leaner hoped.
   "I wouldn't count on that happening, Thurmond."
   "You don't seem too upset about it."
   "Why should I be? As you know, it's best to get all
those antagonistic feelings out of your system. There's
no place for bitterness and hatred on a golf course."
   "Very funny."

The doors of the club swung open, and Catalina and his entourage strutted inside like they owned the place, which of course they did. Catalina was flanked by the Fenners on either side, his brother-in-law Leo carrying Catalina's bullhorn, and Joey caddying for his uncle as punishment for his miserable comedy monologue. Bringing up the rear was Margot. The lighting in the club was more harsh and cruel than the cabin's had been, and Margot looked like a gun moll in an old Cagney movie.

All of this Catalina crew looked like gangsters, when Leaner thought about it.... What if he got caught up with the syndicate when all he was trying to do was to break into the pro ranks? They would have him until he no longer served a purpose, entering him in the pro circuit only to take all his money to invest in casinos, drugs and prostitution.

"Are you hotshots ready to play some golf?" Catalina shouted, disrupting Leaner's anxiety attack, and just when it was getting colorful.

The club customers hooted, jeered, laughed or kept quiet, depending on their early-morning mood. "Ready, willing and *able*," Sherman yelled.

"Will you knock it off?" Leaner said to him. "It's six in the morning."

Catalina climbed one of the chairs, then stepped onto a table to make an announcement. He looked ridiculous up there, and nothing he could say could possibly add as much dignity as standing on a table in an old-time golf outfit took away from him.

"First of all, boys, good luck to each and every one of you. As you know, this is it, the moment I live for, and it wouldn't be possible without your attendance and support. For those of you too nervous to remember when you tee off"—Catalina hesitated, rotating on his heel to catch everyone's eyes—"and for you members of the press, those times are posted on the door of the club. Now, with the help of Mister Sherman, Mister Reasoner, and Mister Leaner, this year's Catalina Invitational will be under way."

"That's us, Bubba," Sherman said.

"Oh, shut up," Leaner said, as Sherman—still playing the fool to mask the killer inside—bounded toward Catalina to aid his climb down from the table.

Leaner lifted his bag, but before he was able to swing it to his shoulder he felt a restraining hand. It was Jonah. Leaner didn't know where he had come from, but felt he was never so glad to see anyone in his life.

"I will carry these," Jonah said. "I am the caddy, you are the pro."

"Jonah," Leaner said. "You don't know how you've come through for me. If I do well in the tournament you get a fat bonus, by George. I mean, here I was a minute ago, really just a bundle of Florida nerves, I don't mind saying. And you showing up on time and as scheduled like you did, well, it's had a great calming effect. You're the only one I can count on up here, and that's the truth. It doesn't make any difference if you know one club from another. Just tilt the bag my way and I'll help myself. We'll be a good team. Just because my life is falling to pieces is no reason to think my golf game isn't on the money...."

Leaner's jittery speech was lost on Jonah, who had been awake until four in the morning snorting cocaine with Joey Fenner and some of the other caddies in the barracks. While Leaner rambled, Jonah felt like he could run with the clubs on his shoulder several times around the course without a breather. Cocaine was something he'd never tried with the pinheads on the farm. The other caddies had never met anyone quite like Jonah and they were all more than willing to corrupt him. Jonah just smiled away during Leaner's verbal rampage.

Leaner was hesitant to join Catalina because of Margot, but she had seated herself at a table nearby, hunched over a cup of coffee by the time he had finished welcoming Jonah.

Leaner felt suddenly marvelous. He knew it was inappropriate, but there was too much going on to analyze why. He left the rest of his breakfast on his table and strolled over to Catalina to see if there were any last-minute opening-round instructions he had dreamed up. Maybe Catalina would set off a fireworks display to mark the opening, or at least shoot a flare over the first fairway—anything to illuminate the dawn. But this was wild wishful thinking. Canoes and Scrabble were Catalina's ideas of extravagance, and the inconvenience of darkness was just an additional hazard Leaner decided he had to play away from. Perhaps he could stall.

"Ray, what do you make of today's weather?" Catalina asked, once the foursome and their caddies were outside.

Ray Reasoner looked to the treetops. He would have been seeing clouds had there been more light. "I'm glad you asked me that, Max," he said. "It will be clear to partly cloudy, with a low in the low sixties and a high in the upper eighties. These fair skies are the result of a high pressure weather system, and they extend across the state. Light and variable surface winds will hold these pleasant conditions in our area for the remainder of the week."

Leaner was dumbfounded by his new partner. It seemed Catalina had a knack for assembling every nut who knew how to hold a golf club. They walked to the first tee, thirty or forty yards from the clubhouse. Leaner didn't remember how long the first hole was and had to consult his scorecard for its length. He thought he could make out a flag somewhere in the distance, but he couldn't be certain that what he saw was even a part of the course. It was just too dark. Catalina teed up.

"A fair warning, boys," he said. "I know this course so well I could play it in the dark."

"You *are* playing it in the dark," Leaner said.

No comment.

Joey Fenner now handed Catalina his driver, part of an ancient set of wooden-shafted clubs that went by such quaint names as brassies and spoons. They were unnumbered, which rattled Leaner a bit. It seemed a backward way to play. It was like fishing with a hand line.

Catalina swung, and his ball disappeared into the darkness. Fenner stood to the side to announce with the bullhorn as the players prepared themselves. "FROM RACINE, WISCONSIN, COSMO SHER-MAN."

Sherman teed up, and Leaner's anxiety ballooned. He went over to Margot. Maybe she could influence her grandfather.

"Margot, ask him to wait. Ask him to postpone this

thing for twenty minutes. Fifteen, at least."

"Why should I? After the awful way you spoke to me this morning. I'm mad at you."

Leaner hissed in a hoarse whisper. "Who do you think you are? Princess Caroline of Monaco, for God's sake?"

Sherman's shot flew away and out of sight. Catalina applauded.

"I'm not kidding," Leaner went on, watching Ray Reasoner tee up. "I really can't see a thing out here. The only reason these other guys are starting is to humor your grandfather."

"RAY REASONER, OF GREENSBORO, NORTH CAROLINA," Fenner boomed.

Reasoner's shot joined Sherman's in the darkness. Margot crossed her arms and turned away from Leaner. Catalina faced them now. "What's the holdup over there?" he asked. "Honey pie, don't bother the players. They have work to do."

Leaner approached Catalina. "Mister Catalina, I must protest these conditions."

"HAILING FROM HOUSTON, TEXAS, ROOKIE THURMOND LEANER."

"You see, the problem is, it's just too dark. I don't want you to think I'm a complainer, but I think not waiting for the sun to come up could be a real disadvantage to the first foursome or two."

Catalina couldn't believe his ears. Someone was undermining what he was living for. He seethed, speechless.

"THURMOND LEANER, OF HOUSTON, TAKE YOUR SHOT."

"What do you say, Mister Catalina? Can we wait a few minutes, or can I play in a later foursome, or what?"

Catalina fought to control himself. "Will you abide by the steward's decision?"

"Sure," Leaner said. "An independent point of view might be just what we need."

"Leo!" Catalina called. "We need your opinion. Can Mister Leaner here play in a later foursome, or must he tee off within the next ninety seconds or face disqualification?"

As soon as Leaner saw that Fenner was the judge, he went for his clubs. He chose a conservative four wood (Catalina's equivalent was called a "spoon"), and said, "I'll play, I'll play." He then grabbed up the bullhorn, held the button on it, and pointed it toward the green. "If there are any people along this fairway, I'd appreciate it if you lit matches or lighters, 'cause I can't see a damn thing out there."

Catalina stared into the darkness, and the lights began to flicker on either side of the fairway like a miniature airport runway. Leaner teed up and hit his drive. It had a smooth, solid feel to it, and he would later find the ball dead center, 240 yards away. Leaner felt remarkably calm; he could have walked a tightrope.

12

LEANER WASN'T THAT BIG
a man. In golf, you didn't have to be. He could hit
remarkable drives, not through the physical strength
of a blacksmith, but with a natural timing and a knowledge of how to attain maximum leverage in his swing
pattern. The first hole on Catalina's course was a night-
mare for those who lacked reasonable distance in their
drives. It was a par-five, 546-yard dogleg to the left
whose green was surrounded by sand traps. Leaner
avoided them successfully and found himself twelve
feet from the pin in regulation three strokes. His concentration over the putt was so intense that the others
in his foursome could have been the Marx brothers and
he wouldn't have cracked a smile. He hit the putt solid
and smooth, right into the bottom of the cup. It gave
him quite a boost to birdie the opening hole, and he
acknowledged with a smile the applause of the meager
gallery as he retrieved the ball.

Sherman bogied, Reasoner made par and Catalina
blasted from one sand trap to another, finishing with

an eleven. By the time he was through, though, there was all the daylight anyone could want.

A fairly straight and unassuming hole, Number Two was a par-four 384-yarder. Leaner could still hear Fenner over the bullhorn in the morning air as the tournament streamed in behind his own foursome. His group teed off, Catalina dribbling his drive, topping the ball scarcely eighty yards. Leaner wanted to think of nothing but his own play but couldn't help worrying over the way Catalina was slowing down the pace. After all, Leaner was leading the tournament, even if there was only one hole behind him. He didn't want to think about what a ten-minute break between shots would do to his momentum. Catalina might as well have been throwing his ball at the hole.

Sherman shanked his drive into the trees, cocking his head sideways like a hound as he watched it vanish from sight.

Reasoner made a nice shot straight down the middle, and Leaner's split the fairway too, as well as outdistancing Reasoner by forty yards. After that shot, Catalina said, "I have the feeling, Thurmond, you're the man in this tournament to watch."

"I think so too," Margot chirped, puckering her mouth at him, pumping her hips, a look of absolute deprivation in her eyes.

Ignore them all, Leaner told himself, handing his club to Jonah. The whole family is too eccentric....

Leaner this day was a golf-playing machine, and after the first nine he was a near incredible five under par. He had never played so well, and when he tried to analyze just what he was doing differently he came up with nothing—except days on end of anxiety preceding actual play. Maybe that was what he needed to perform at his peak, and beyond it....

On the twelfth he heard a muffled roar of applause and shouting, and asked Catalina what the commotion could be. Catalina checked his watch. "Buck Hollingsworth must have just teed off," he said.

As they spoke they watched Sherman chopping himself out of the woods. He was already nine over par.

"It's funny," Leaner said as he waited to tee off. "I never saw Hollingsworth at any of the qualifying events."

"That's because he wasn't there," Catalina said. "Names don't have to qualify. You heard the crowd. Names draw the crowds. Let me tell you something in confidence, Thurwood Leaner."

"What's that?"

"You could be a name."

Leaner was silent.

"You have the talent. I've seen you in some tough situations today, and you've handled every one of them like a true name. Believe me, you're a potential *name*."

Sherman's shot from the rough had landed in the middle of a lake. He walked across the fairway and stood at the water's edge, watching the ripples made by his ball, leaning on his club as if it was a cane. Leaner didn't like to see him doing so poorly, in spite of their differences in the early morning. Actually he had gotten to like Sherman, once he began to understand him better. He wanted to help him now, and joined him by the water while Catalina and Ray Reasoner were taking their shots. Sherman was gritting his teeth, and why not? He was playing awful.

"Loosen up," Leaner told him.

"The god-dam bas-tard," Sherman spit out each syllable. He turned around, facing the green where Catalina's convertible was parked. "Catalina, you asshole," he said.

"I hope that helps," Leaner told him. "You know he can't hear you, so it was just for your own benefit."

"I realize that," Sherman smiled. "If only he wouldn't have his funny-boy nephew Joey driving him in that little car of his like something that escaped from Disneyland, he wouldn't get under my skin so much."

It was Leaner's shot now, and he hit an iron five feet from the cup and added yet another birdie. He almost felt like apologizing to Sherman. He also felt that his game would suddenly blow up on him.

But it never did. He had endless patience, waited out Catalina's pitiful play, mostly ignored Margot's distractions in the background, and even put himself on hold for over a minute when he felt a sneeze coming on when he was about to putt. He had fouled up a shot in Florida once because of a sneeze, and had sworn never to let another one take him by surprise.

By the 514-yard eighteenth, Leaner was seven under par. Word had spread through the gallery how well he was playing, and there was quite a crowd gathered at the last hole, filling the bleachers and spilling onto the fairway near the green.

The tee shot had to clear a portion of the canoe lake and land on the fairway between two bunkers. Leaner played it perfectly. He was on the green with a two wood, leaving him a thirty-foot putt for an eagle.

While waiting for the others to make the green he had a sneezing attack. So far as he knew, his only allergy was to mangoes, but no doubt there were all sorts of pollen and dust and crud in the Catskills that he had never breathed in Texas. He walked slowly to the green, swinging the putter like a scythe through imaginary knee-deep weeds. Squatting to line up the putt, he told himself, "My luck held for one day. It's more than I expected."

He missed the putt but canned the remaining three-footer for another birdie. Margot ran to him, kissing him sloppily in full view of the grandstand.

"Honey pie!" Catalina exclaimed, and shook his head.

Leaner still had hold of his putter, and used it as a wedge, so to speak, between himself and Margot. He turned now, handing the club to Jonah. "Take care of the clubs, will you? You were great. Thanks a lot." Actually the kid did seem to catch on fast, as he had promised.

Leaner felt another sneeze cresting like a wave within him as he handed over the putter to Jonah. He turned away, facing sideways, and blasted into the lens of a camera. "Excuse me," he said. "It's very crowded here."

"That's all right," the man with the camera said. "It'll make a good picture. I'm John Randall from the Utica *Tribune.* Can we talk about that round you just finished?"

"I don't mind," Leaner said.

"Fine. I'll just keep you a minute. I understand this is your first tournament."

"That's right," Leaner said. "As a pro, anyway. As a matter of fact, it's the first I've played competitively in about six months."

"Why is that?"

"I didn't see much point in playing for free any more and I just turned pro. I'm ready."

"That must be some feeling."

"It's exciting," Leaner said. "There's no question about it. It opens all kinds of possibilities."

Sherman joined them now to see who Leaner was talking to, and Leaner introduced them. "This is Cosmo Sherman. He made up four strokes in the last six holes."

Sherman and the reporter nodded to each other.

"One more question. There seems to be a tradition in golf: Fuzzy Zoeller, Tom Kite, Bruce Lietzke, Hale Irwin, Andy Bean, Ben Crenshaw, Orville Moody, Miller Barber, Buck Hollingsworth, Howard Twitty, Rod Curl, Kermit Zarley and so on. Even as far back as Byron Nelson, Sam Snead and Max Catalina. What do all these guys have in common?"

Leaner was pensive. Then: "They're all names?"

"They're all *funny* names," the reporter said. "Why, hell, look at you two. Thurmond and Cosmo. Leaner and Sherman. You even sound like a couple of clowns—"

"I think that's enough," Leaner said.

The reporter puffed his face up like a red blowfish. "What are you gonna do?" he said. "Beat me up? Gun me down?"

Leaner suddenly thought of the father of the snotty kid he'd met on the road. "There's a potential danger in talking to a stranger," he said calmly. "It's like farting when you have diarrhea."

"Let me take him," Sherman blurted out, lunging for Randall's camera strap to choke him.

Leaner pulled him off. "Nobody's going to take anybody. I merely meant, Mister Randall, that you might think you know what you're doing, but you could very well get the shit knocked out of you if you keep it up. Now, good-day to you."

John Randall laughed unpleasantly in their faces and disappeared into the crowd. "One more nut has surfaced in the Catskills," Leaner told Sherman.

"You should have let me take him," Sherman said. "I know I could take him."

A boy of about ten carrying a baseball approached Leaner. "Can you autograph my ball?"

Leaner smiled. A first. "All right, what would you like me to write?"

"To Freddie, good luck. Then sign your name. What *is* your name, anyway?"

"Thurmond Leaner."

The boy thought a minute. "Would you mind just signing it Reggie Jackson?" he asked, and Leaner did without missing a beat. Another wise-ass kid, he thought.

Leaner now haunted the eighteenth green area, blending in with the gallery there to watch his competition as they finished up their rounds. Then he decided that the best thing he could do for his sinuses was to vacuum pack himself inside the cabin and run the air conditioner. He managed to elude Margot by squirming his way through the crowds.

Back in the cabin he filled a glass of water at the little kitchenette sink, peeled off his shirt and draped it around his neck. He was extremely pleased with the way he had played the opening round and, try as he might to not think of the implications, he was too happy and excited not to—his score had finally sunk in. He also ached a little in his arms, and his head felt like one big sinus cavity. He knew he had to eat something, but there was no way to get anything down. He felt like jumping on the bed to celebrate, but self-conscious even in private, he restricted himself to a face-stretching grin.

He would share the news with Lauren.

"Thurmond?" she said. "I was just thinking about you. I thought you'd be playing right about now."

"I'm on Eastern time," Leaner said. "Anyway, I teed off at the crack of dawn and finished about an hour ago."

"So how did it go?"

"Pretty good," he said. "Great, in fact. I shot a sixty-three, babe. *Eight under par.* I'm leading the tournament, but a lot of guys haven't finished yet."

"My God," Lauren said. "What's first place money up there?"

"I think it's thirty-five thousand. Maybe forty. That's getting a little ahead of ourselves to talk money, Lauren. It looks like I'll bring home something, though."

"That's a lot of pressure to be under. It's more money than you've made in the past two years. No wonder we've been biting each other's heads off every time we talk.... Well, I have some good news too. I know you're not thrilled about the idea of having a monkey, but I've found the saddle, and Bingo took his first ride yesterday evening."

"Where did he go?"

"Don't get smart, Thurmond. This is the love of your life you're talking to. Your reason for living, remember?"

"I remember," he said.

"I had the dog on a length of rope, and Bingo on another one. Then the dog tried to tree a squirrel, and they both got a little tangled up. I straightened it out again and found the trick is to get the dog to do all the work. All Bingo really has to do is hang on. I really think it's the second or third funniest thing I've ever seen. I can just imagine it when Bingo's in his outfit."

"Sure, honey, sure..."

She paused. Leaner could see her inhaling slowly to belt him with a few well-thrown and forceful retorts.

"Can't you *see?*" she said. "I'm doing the same thing you are. It's the lure of making money, without the work routine."

"I hadn't thought of it like that," Leaner said.

"Am I right, or am I crazy?" Lauren asked him. "Never mind, I'd rather not know."

"Lauren, do you want to fly up and meet me here for the rest of the tournament? I miss you, and everybody up here is beginning to get on my nerves. It's a real mess, and the only good thing that's happened is my score today."

"We can't count on any money until you're through up there, and I'd hate to spend what we don't have. Besides, you'll be home in a week."

"Maybe not," Leaner said. "I may go to Boston."

"Boston? You never said Boston before."

"Amelia gave me the name of an agent there. I thought I'd drop in and introduce myself. I might be able to line up an endorsement if I do well here in the Catskills."

"That's great. Why hadn't you mentioned it before now?"

"It's nothing firm," Leaner said. "And I'd sort of forgotten it myself until I ran across Amelia's note in my shaving kit."

"I'd better stay here," Lauren said. "I have the animals to take care of. I think you should see that agent, though."

"I probably will," Leaner said. "I'll talk with you soon, then. I love you."

"Thank you," Lauren said.

Leaner said goodbye and hung up, then undressed for the shower.

It felt good under the water, and he stayed there until it began to run cold. He cleared a place on the mirror, combed his hair and walked toward his suitcase at the foot of his bed—where Margot was stretched out, altogether at home.

"How did you get in here? I know I locked the door. Did Fenner give you a key?"

"This reminds me of the day we met," Margot said. "It was so romantic."

"Margot, please get out of my life. I'm not cruel by nature, but I can't think of a way to make it any clearer. Just *beat* it, okay?"

"As I recall, you were leaving the shower over there"—she gestured—"and I was here, like where I am now."

Leaner pulled on his pants and put on a shirt. "You have a great memory," he said. "That was all of two days ago and you can remember it like it was yesterday. Margot, please. Get dressed and just leave."

"You couldn't resist me then and you can't resist me now."

"What will it take to convince you? I am not interested in you. I was horny, and horniness is no basis for a relationship"—God, how stuffy he sounded.... Well, he couldn't help it, he had to get her out of there, didn't he?

Without another word she slipped on her clothes and stepped through the doorway. He lay down on the bed and stayed inside all day, leaving only for dinner. He felt like a salesman on the road. Around ten Margot knocked on his door, and Leaner admitted her, gladly.

In the morning he was under the covers like an animal in its burrow, with Margot prodding him into consciousness by running her fingernails lightly over his ribs, which made his skin crawl. It bothered him...it was the same trick that Lauren used on him at home.

"Don't you love me just a little?" she was saying. "Not even a tiny bit?"

Leaner opened one eye. "What do you want from me?" he said. "It's not enough that you have my body. You're after my alleged soul with a fly swatter. And please, lay off the ribs."

"My man is ticklish," Margot said. "And in the mornings, a little bit mean."

Leaner got up from the bed to brush his teeth. He watched himself in the mirror. True, he never sought Margot out, but the fact that he kept accepting her made him feel weak-willed as a puppy. He wanted the tournament to be done with, regardless of how he finished, just so he could leave the Catskills. It was as if something in the air affected not only his sinuses, but produced mental sneezes as well.

An awful pounding, so loud that it had to be an emergency, threatened to knock down his front door while he rinsed his mouth. His first thought being to conceal

Margot, he burst out of the bathroom.

"Quick," he said. "Into the bathroom."

"I think not," Margot said, sitting up in the bed.

Leaner put on some pants and opened the door a crack. "Who is it?"

"Leo Fenner."

"What do you need, *Fenner*?" He hoped Margot would take the cue.

"Max wants you in his office right away."

"What does he want?"

"All I know is he told me to come and get you, and not to come back without you, so let's go."

"I want to practice my putting first," Leaner said. "Tell him I'll meet him in half an hour."

Fenner craned his neck to look inside. "Max can't wait. Is my niece in there with you?"

"Just let me throw on a shirt," Leaner said evasively. He picked up his shirt, squeezed through the door and locked it.

They got into Catalina's convertible, and Fenner drove straight to the club. He led Leaner up a flight of stairs, pushed open a door for him, then closed it behind him.

Leaner assumed this had something to do with screwing the daylights out of Catalina's granddaughter, and he didn't much blame Catalina if that was it. Maybe it was just the excuse Leaner was needing for Margot.... "I'm sorry, I can't see you anymore. Your grandfather won't let me." It sounded too wimpy.

A picture window overlooked the golf course, and Leaner had a good view of the first and tenth tees from behind Catalina's desk. He watched a foursome begin the back nine but became anxious and walked across the office to inspect the photographs covering one wall.

It was a pictorial history of Catalina's illustrious golf career. There he stood accepting the trophy for winning the British Open, here he shook hands with Dwight Eisenhower in a sand trap. In another he sat side-by-side with Bob Hope in a golf cart. As the pictures progressed from left to right, Catalina aged—gracefully, Leaner had to admit. Beside the door a youthful Catalina with tar-black hair stood arm-in-arm with someone Leaner recognized but couldn't quite place. He thought it might be Charles Lindbergh.

Catalina entered, smoking a cigar, a newspaper folded under one arm. He walked briskly past Leaner, dropped the paper on the desk and sat in his chair. "Sit," he said, gesturing across the desk. "Please, sit."

Leaner was embarrassed that Catalina had to put himself through this, and that he had gotten in the situation with Margot to begin with. He started to make an opening remark but restrained himself to hear Catalina out first.

"Have you seen today's paper?" Catalina asked, pushing it toward Leaner. "If you haven't, you should. You got some write-up there."

In bold headlines on the front of the sports page, Leaner saw: HOLLINGSWORTH IN SECOND WITH 67. Below this, practically in parentheses, he read: "Rookie Leaner First Round Leader."

"That's nice," Leaner said. "Thank you for showing it to me."

"Turn the page."

Leaner opened up the section to see two pictures of himself on page three. One was of him sneezing, the other of Margot embracing him at the end of the round.

He read the caption out loud: "Rookie Thurmond Leaner celebrates a first-round lead in the Catalina Invitational (left) by attacking woman bystander, un-identified. When confronted (right) he spits at photographer." Leaner reread the item to himself. "Mister Catalina, I really don't know what to think about this. You know it's all a lie, don't you?"

"Of course," Catalina said. "Muckraking is nothing new. I've experienced this kind of thing before."

"How do you handle it?"

"It's best to ignore it, because by denying the lie, or even referring to it, you lend it truth. I won't comment on it if I'm asked by the media. But the damage is already done. Hopefully, the fire will die down. Then again, it might spread. There's an article in there too, by a John Randall."

"That's the guy who gave me a hard time."

"What he wrote is garbage," Catalina said. "Turn the page."

The head on the article read: "Bad Boy in a Gentleman's Game." He scanned it. Randall wrote that he would like to quote Leaner for the paper, but his vocabulary would embarrass a Marine drill instructor. He went on to say that Leaner was semiliterate, anti-Semitic and unpatriotic.

"Go ahead, you can take the paper with you," Catalina said. "And good luck today."

"Thanks." Leaner headed for the door, remembered the photo on the wall. "Is that Lindbergh?" he asked.

Catalina was walking him to the door. "Let's see. I don't have on my glasses. Which one do you mean?"

"That one." Leaner pointed.

Catalina took out his glasses from his pocket and

held them away from his face. "No, Lindbergh's over there. That's Calvin Coolidge you're looking at."

"Oh? Well, thanks again," Leaner said. The old man, of course, had them reversed.

"One more thing. You might not have noticed. Those pictures in the paper?"

"Yes?"

"They're wire service. You're probably in about six hundred newspapers today. You may not be a name yet, but with that sort of exposure, I'll guarantee one thing."

"What's that?"

"You're a face, Thurmond Leaner."

13

LEANER COULDN'T FIND FENNER
to catch a ride back to his cabin. He wasn't angry about
being summoned, just resentful about the unfair publicity. He talked to himself all the way to the cabin.

"First there was Florida. Then I had to drive halfway
across the continent. There was that kid, and then Kid
Doolin. I listened to Joey Fenner's monologue, played
Scrabble and rowed a canoe. I was a good goddamn
sport. I had a great opening round. And what do I get
for it? A punch in the mouth. Millions of readers now
think I spit at people and attack women. Is my fling
with Catalina's honey pie to blame? If that's the case,
why is retribution so swift? Turn the page, he kept
saying, and it got worse and worse with every new page.
I can only hope that it's over now...."

He opened the cabin door and Margot rushed to him,
not in her usual lustful urgency but with genuine fear
molding her expression.

"Was granddaddy mad?"

"No, grandda—, I mean, Catalina—was not mad. He

151

wanted me to see this." He showed Margot the photo of her kissing Leaner.

"Unidentified bystander?" she said. "This guy has some nerve! I'd have told him my name *and* who I was if he'd asked. I'd have said, 'I'm Margot Catalina, Leaner's woman.'"

"I should be thankful for small blessings," Leaner said.

"I don't care who sees it," Margot said. "What do I care? If love is mad, then I'm mad."

Leaner was sitting on the foot of the bed, staring out the window. "I would think that you'd be upset that the photographs and article are a pack of lies rather than over the omission of your name from the mudslinging."

Margot looked at him, as though thinking on what Leaner had said. Finally... "If I were Japanese and you were a GI, would you take me home as your war bride?"

"For God's sake, will you get out of here?"

He shoved her outside and tossed her shoes after her. A few minutes passed, and he heard a light rapping on the door. "I told you to get the—" But it was Jonah, hat in hand, trembling.

"I didn't mean you," Leaner said. "Come on in."

Jonah sat on the couch he had recently slept on and looked about the room.

"So how are things in the barracks?" Leaner asked him, trying to soothe his nerves.

"It is a fine barracks."

"Good, that's good... you realize that these cabins really just accommodate one person?"

"The barracks is a fine place for the caddies."

"Right," Leaner said. "I think we've just about exhausted that subject. Did you need to see me about something? We tee off at ten today."

"I came to ask whether you saw our appearance in the newspaper."

"I sure did," Leaner said, tossing Jonah the sports section.

"Two pictures," Jonah said with surprise. "My paper showed only one."

"Which paper?"

"It is the one the boy Joey bought, from New York City."

"The *Times*?"

"Yes, the New York *Times*."

Leaner sighed. "They have world-wide circulation. Did you say 'we?'"

"Yes." Jonah pointed. "I appear in the pictures carrying your clubs."

Leaner took another look. "I don't know why I didn't notice you before."

"Are my duties the same as yesterday?"

"Just meet me at the course at ten," Leaner said, then added, "Are you positive you don't want a new shirt?"

Jonah shook his head and left the cabin.

"I never used to raise my voice at people," Leaner said aloud.

He felt his sinuses begin to close again and ran to his car. He drove raggedly to the grocery in Roscoe, bought some nonprescription allergy medicine and rushed back to the tournament. He wanted to scream at the line of traffic leading to the golf course, passing them illegally on the right. He stopped by the cabin for his shoes and sprinted to the course, certain that his foursome had teed off and he was disqualified. It turned out that he had plenty of time. He made it to the first tee a little winded but punctual. It distressed him to see Catalina there, since it was rumored that he would only play in the opening round. Maybe he was on hand only to see everyone off, like a senile king putting his armada to sea.

"I know what I said yesterday, Max," Ray Reasoner was apologizing to Catalina, "but those light and variable surface winds have changed direction. They're sweeping in from the Atlantic now, and scattered thundershowers are prevailing along the upper seaboard. Boston has had a half-inch of rain, and New York City, while dry at the moment, can't escape the effects of the same weather system. We've just got to watch that barometric pressure. The barometric pressure is the key to whether we stay dry or not."

Catalina listened, nodding now and then. "Thanks for keeping me posted, Ray."

Leaner hadn't spoken to Reasoner except for an occasional compliment on a shot the day before. He wondered if meteorology was a hobby of his.

"How did you get to be a weatherman?" Leaner asked him.

"Down in Greensboro, I do the weather on a TV station. I'm on vacation now."

"That's interesting," Leaner said. "Seems most sports personalities, when they end up on television, always do the sports reporting."

"I took what I could get," Reasoner said sullenly.

"Are you any relation to Harry Reasoner?"

"Not that I know of."

"Well, is it going to rain?"

Reasoner's forehead drew up into a road map of wrinkles. "Those two questions are all anyone ever asks me," he said with disappointment, lowering his head and walking away.

"What a melancholy meteorologist." "Sherman," Leaner said, turning around, "I didn't hear you sneak up."

"You also didn't see or hear any reporters. Catalina's put a gag on the press. I've seen you in six papers so far, and you come across like Hitler with a nine iron."

"It's terrible," Leaner admitted, "but I'm just going to try to ignore it all. Catalina seems to think that would be for the best too, which I assume is why he doesn't want any journalists around."

"Sounds to me like there's something to hide. The club and cabins are the only unrestricted areas for the press. I don't know, excluding the press from a golf tournament? And all because of you."

"But I didn't do anything—"

"That's a pretty convincing photograph. There's no question that it's you and you look like you're spitting right at the camera."

"That was a *sneeze*, I'm allergic to something up here." He pulled out a nasal spray and took a good dose in each nostril, then made a pitiful expression, as if his head was packed with mercury and sand.

Sherman looked at him dubiously. The foursome ahead of them was on the first green now and it was time for him to tee off. Sherman's first round score was 77, which put him under a strain but not out of contention. He was among a pack tied for eighth place.

* * *

Leaner birdied two of the first four holes, making par on the others. By the fifth hole he felt he should let loose and tap his reserves. He had been holding back because of the allergy, thinking he might have nothing left for the back nine unless he took it easy.

Number Five was the shortest hole on the course, a plain vanilla 180-yard par-three with a puddle of a lake to the right of the green. Sherman and Reasoner both hit the green without complication. Leaner plucked and tossed some grass blades, watching the effect of the wind on them as they fell. The wind seemed to be with him. He tightened his glove and imagined the shot just as he would like it to be. He nodded to Jonah and selected a six iron—

His concentration abruptly sputtered as he thought of Margot, canoe racing, eight-by-ten framed pictures of Catalina, and possible libel trials. He shook his head slightly, closed his eyes to shut out the distracting images. He took his backswing, eyes held the ball, downswing, locating the ball after his follow-through, floating, then closed his eyes again against a bitter sneeze erupting from deep inside him, one that could turn a lung inside out, and out it came with an explosion that merged with the noise of the gallery. There were screams, he was clapped on the back and jostled. He looked for the ball on the green but had trouble finding it.

In fact, the ball had landed six feet past the pin, backspin taking it right to the lip of the cup. The crowd tried to cheer it in. Leaner strode to the green, basking in the love of the gallery. Even the hostile press should now sing a different tune. He wished he had Catalina's bullhorn to rally them, but by the time he got to the green, putter in hand, his priorities had changed. He dropped his club and cupped his hands around his mouth.

"Is there an allergist in the gallery?" he shouted, and the crowd suddenly became faces on the deck of a passing ship, silent spectators once more, distant, drained of enthusiasm. Even annoyed. Leaner tapped in his ball to sparse applause.

"You had 'em there for a minute," Ray Reasoner told him.

"Yes I did," Leaner said, projecting his next drive in his head.

"But you lost 'em."

"They can go fuck themselves," Leaner said, exchanging his putter for a driver with Jonah. "And so can you—wait, I didn't mean that. A lot of stuff is happening all at once to me, I can't handle it too easily. Sorry..."

Mass approval wasn't foremost in Leaner's mind, but given the choice he wouldn't mind having people on his side. A legion of fans lining the fairways would be a definite boost. Still, the numbers that had turned out this day said something. The gallery around him had grown substantially in only one day, as if yeast had been added to the dough overnight. That said something, didn't it? Yeah, but maybe it was just that they had come to watch him spit on somebody.

With this, his third bird in five holes, he was increasing his lead. He faced the decision now either to continue his steady game plan, hoping for the stray advance on par, or to play all out. There would be a danger of overplaying the shots. He knew from experience that his control was a little wild when he tried to play catch-up. But Leaner was in command of his game. Everything felt right. He decided to make a charge.

Number Six was a longish par-four, 410 yards, with traps strung the length of the right side of the fairway and, on the left, a peninsula of boulders extending into the field of play about halfway to the tee. The previous day Leaner had been intimidated by that pile of rocks out there. This time, he intended to keep clear of them to the right.

It was his worst shot of the tournament, the ball landing squarely in one of the right-hand bunkers. Leaner stepped out of the way of his playing partners, stood quietly to the side as they made their shots, then asked Sherman whether he had seen what he'd done.

"Maybe the level of competition pulled you down."

"Come on, that's not an answer."

"I wasn't watching," Sherman said.

Reasoner, whose feelings had been hurt on the previous hole, offered no comment.

Leaner surveyed the situation. He was still 230 yards from the flag and in a trap. At least the ball hadn't plugged itself beneath the surface. It had taken a bounce and lay on a stretch of sand that was packed hard like a beach. "I screwed up, Jonah," he told his caddy. "Hand me that four wood. That one over there."

Leaner pulled the wood out of his bag when Jonah didn't act quickly enough to suit him. He had never tried a wood from the sand before, but since he had decided to play out the round hell-bent for leather, he might as well give it a shot. If it looked like showboating, then so be it. He had a good lie, and if he could manage to make contact without bulldozing a scoop of sand on his downswing, he calculated that he had a fair chance of making the green. He wasn't aiming for the pin. Anywhere within fifty feet of it would suit him fine.

He set his feet in the sand, anchoring his position well up past the soles of his shoes. He wound back and swung as hard as he could, grunting like a two-handed tennis player on a hard volley. The ball sailed low, took a big bounce and rolled to the edge of the green, then took a bounce on a hidden obstacle and stopped twelve feet from the flag.

Sherman was standing out of Leaner's line of sight behind him. "That was something," he said. "I've never seen a shot like that in my life. Not by Buck Hollingsworth, not even by Sam Snead, or anybody."

"It was just one shot," Leaner told him as they separated on the fairway. One in a million, he added to himself.

He was riding high and sitting pretty. He punched the air, shadowboxing his concealed enemies—Catalina, Florida, his cousin Vernon. Someone in the gallery shouted out, "All *right,*" and Leaner wheeled around in the direction of the voice, bowing his head in appreciation.

When it was his turn he charged the green, putter in hand. He walked a circle around the ball, could feel the grain of the grass with his feet. He squatted once to confirm it, lined up and aimed. He drew back without hesitation, sank the twelve-footer with confidence and threw his arms into the air, tossing the putter to Jonah.

With Five and Six birdied, Leaner had strung together four sub-par holes in succession. By the time he reached the back nine he was seven under for the day. He felt as if he were a gladiator. Word of his remarkable playing had spread through the ranks, and at each successive hole the crowds were thicker, louder and more encouraging. He liked the way the applause traveled through the body of the gallery in waves, like wind crossing a field of tall grass. He strained at every hole. He gave them their money's worth. It was as if nothing could go wrong if he maintained his intensity, his momentum (that overworked word, but it applied). He did have some breaks, too. Putts were dropping as if the balls were equipped with homing devices. One poor tee shot ricocheted off a tree into the middle of the fairway. Leaner felt blessed. Maybe the canoes, the Scrabble, the infidelity to Lauren were just what he needed to hone the rough edges from Catalina's course. The Catskills were being pretty good to him after all.

On the course nothing else intruded on his problem solving, which in large part was what the game was to him—a series of problems to overcome, brain teasers. The lie of the ball, the wind direction, the plane of the fairway—they were all components of the jigsaw puzzle. When a fairway doglegged sharply, Leaner shifted his stance just right from open to closed, whatever it took, and made the precise adjustment in his grip, moving the ball from left to right as though he had a magically extended arm controlling it. It was eerie.

He ended the round tying the Catalina record with a ten-under 61. As the final putt dropped, his feet sprung him up over the hole. He came down on one knee, drew himself up and handed the putter to Jonah. The impromptu celebration was a crowd pleaser, and when Leaner realized that the cheering was in response to

his acrobatics, it made him self-conscious. He composed himself, dismissed his caddy and carried his golf
bag to the cabin. Now, for the first time, he began to
comprehend that he might actually run away with the
tournament. One thing he had decided was that whoever
did win would have to take it away from him. He wasn't
going to give it away.

He was stopped from approaching his cabin by a covey
of reporters camped outside the steps to the front door.
One guy was even sitting on the hood of his parked
car. He slipped among them, setting down his bag as
he got out the key to the cabin.

"Do you have a statement?" one of them demanded,
sounding hostile.

"Yes," Leaner said, "please let me through—"

"No, no," the reporter said. "A statement on what
happened yesterday afternoon, on your behavior after
the first round."

"Look, fellas," Leaner said, "I'll talk about golf all
you want. I did have quite a round today. Give me an
hour to clean up and unwind and I'll meet you in the
club. I'll buy you all a round of beers—"

"How about the girl, the spitting..."

Leaner pushed his way through and locked himself
inside. Maybe he was a little too quick to suggest a
meeting in the bar. If he got the press liquored up they
could really turn on him. He took a quick shower, heard
the phone ringing as he turned off the water.

"You were in the *Houston Post*," Lauren said. "Who's
your new girlfriend?"

"Lauren, regardless of what the caption may be on
the picture you saw, what happened was just a spon-
taneous, congratulatory kind of thing that people up

here do. That was just Mister Catalina's little grand-daughter Margot."

"She looks full grown to me," Lauren said.

"Well, she is, but she hasn't outgrown that childlike enthusiasm for off-the-cuff displays of..."

"Are you still there, Thurmond?"

"Yes, I just couldn't think of how to finish that sentence. This allergy really has hold of me. I was really exhausted on the last two or three holes today. I tied the course record, and I'm eighteen under par now."

Lauren whooped in delight. Leaner was thankful that he had swung the conversation away from the subject of Margot, but felt that if he kept talking it would have to come up again and he didn't want that. "I really ought to go," he said. "I don't want my sinuses to get out of hand."

He hadn't had two minutes to himself when Fenner began knocking on his door. The reporters had left. Fenner couldn't see clearly inside and pressed his face against the glass of the door to catch a glimpse of Leaner.

"Are you in there? Hello?"

Leaner swung the door open suddenly and extended his hand, vigorously shaking Fenner's, hoping to divert him by this abrupt show of hearty friendliness. "Mister Catalina wants to see me again."

"That's true," Fenner said, trying to get his hand back. "How did you know?"

"Where there's smoke, there's fire. I'll be able to join him in a few minutes but I'm afraid it's out of the question for me to leave immediately."

"But I'm not supposed to come back without you. Max was very specific. Can I have my hand back?"

Leaner released his hand. "Consider your message delivered."

"Do you mind if I wait for you? Max would skin me alive if I didn't bring you in."

"For Christ's sake, Fenner, you sound like a bounty hunter."

Leaner closed and locked the door. He ate a sandwich, drank a glass of water. When he felt he'd waited long enough to make his point, he walked outside in the direction of Catalina's office at the club, stopping once and looking over his shoulders, catching Fenner, who quickly pretended to be tying his shoelaces.

The office was open but empty. Leaner was drawn again to the wall of pictures and this time studied what looked like a shot of Catalina posed on an oceanside golf course with the late Generalissimo Francisco Franco.

"We took a poll," Catalina said from the hall outside, then walked to his desk with a sheaf of papers.

Leaner said nothing.

"First of all, Thurmond Leaner, let me say that you played beautifully today. It was above my expectations of you, and came as a complete surprise."

"I think there's a compliment in there," Leaner said. "Thank you."

"Thirdly, attendance is—"

"Secondly," Leaner pointed out. "You left out secondly, I think."

Catalina clenched a cigar he had been chewing and struck a match. "Let's skip numbers and get down to brass tacks," he said as he lit the cigar. "You, Thurmond Leaner, are boosting attendance. Our poll shows there's no question. A market research outfit just got the figures in for me and the figures don't lie. The results: about half the gallery live or vacation in the Catskills. They would show up anyway, because the Invitational is the only sports event except horseracing inside a two-hour drive of here. Another twenty percent are on hand to catch Buck Hollingsworth in action. I told you about names already. What I'm getting at is, eight percent have you and only you in mind when they buy their ticket of admission. You're the reason they came to Roscoe, New York."

"I have a cousin who sells Christmas trees," Leaner said. "One sale has to last him the year. I guess it's the same with you."

Catalina rolled right along. "We had seventy-five hundred through the gates yesterday, and nine thousand today," he beamed, jotting on a piece of paper. "Eight percent of nine thousand is seven hundred and twenty. That many people came out to see you. How does that make you feel?"

"Okay, but I'm not sure what your point is."

"I'll lay it out for you. Another part of the survey, what they call the analysis, shows that by the time a spectator buys his ticket, pays for accessories—I like to call them excessories—he spends close to fourteen dollars. That's sandwiches, beer, sun visors and the like. Now, here's my point, as you put it. If you bring in seven hundred twenty people today and an additional seven-twenty the remaining rounds, and they each spend fourteen dollars, we're talking about—"

"Goddam," Leaner said, "you're talking about thirty thousand dollars."

"I'm talking about a pretty penny. I bring in a pretty

penny, I pay out a pretty penny in winnings, mainte-
nance and salaries. What I want from you is your promise to attend a press conference at five. That's about
two hours away. If possible, create another scene like
you did after the first round. The press can work with
that, and it's bound to help attendance even more. It
just might be all that's needed to make a *name* for
yourself. And then the sky's the limit."

"What happened to your theory of ignoring the whole
thing and it would go away?"

"The research poll showed me wrong, and the figures
don't lie. I must have been wrong."

"The answer is no," Leaner said. "I went along with
the canoe stuff, but pretty penny or no pretty penny, I
can't do it."

Fenner burst into the office. "Sorry to interrupt, Max,
but the periscopes just arrived. I've got Joey unloading
the truck now. Should we tag them at a discount since
they arrived late?"

"Let's see the invoice."

Fenner stepped in front of Leaner and presented
Catalina with the packing list.

"We're getting them for two and a quarter each. We
should be able to move all eight thousand at nine dollars apiece, don't you think, Leo?"

"Seventy-two grand," Leaner said in a monotone.

"They're already lining up for them," Fenner said.

"Fine. Nine dollars it is, then."

Fenner left to manage the periscope business, and
Leaner followed him to the door. "If I show up at five,"
he said, "it will be to try to protect what's left of my
good name—"

"It *is* a good name," Catalina said, not flustered in

the least. "Don't let anyone tell you otherwise."

"Before I go, would you answer something for me?"

"My door is always open," Catalina said. "The club itself may be locked, but my door is open." He said it with a straight face.

Leaner pointed to the picture he'd seen.

"Is that man in the military uniform Francisco Franco?"

Catalina left his desk and joined Leaner, looking down his nose at the picture in question. "No, that's Georgie Jessel," he said.

14

LEANER STARED AT THE
ceiling from his bed, his head flowing with numbers.
If thirty thousand dollars equaled eight percent, he rea-
soned that one percent would be about five thousand.
Then the whole ball of wax, a four-day grab, would net
Catalina close to half a million dollars. "But the cheap
son of a bitch will buy only eight canoes," he said
aloud.

He saw Sherman standing on the porch holding aloft
a six-pack of beer. Leaner gestured for him to come in.

"For my money, you've got this thing all but sewed
up," Sherman told him. "How does it feel?"

"Nothing's sewed up," Leaner said, breaking open
his beer. "Catalina is having a press conference to throw
me to the wolves. He wants me to put on a show, have
a tantrum or a fit or something, figures the publicity
will bring in more people. As if his half million wasn't
enough. You were right all along, Sherman. It sounded
like you had a grudge against the guy, but no question,
Max Catalina has a rotten streak. He's a bad, bad man."

167

"Don't get upset, now," Sherman said. "Drink your beer, and remember the tournament. Just think of the cut you'll take if you only make par from here out."

Leaner took a big swig of beer. "I never thought I'd say this about money, because I've always worked fairly hard for what I've made. I've never had a lot at once. But when you consider the source of this tournament money, whatever the amount, you have to figure it's tainted."

Sherman was incredulous. He set down his drink. "What money isn't?" he said. "Listen to me, friend, if you keep playing like you have been, you can live damn comfortably for probably two years. What's two more days of Catalina against that?"

"I see your point."

"Why do you think I'm here?" Sherman went on. "Do you know what I do the rest of the year? Didn't I tell you I sell insurance and I'm not so good at it? In two weeks, Parkland Life and Casualty has their annual convention. It's in Omaha, of all the godforsaken places, and the company's not paying for our transportation there. If the impossible happened and I finished the Catalina with six month's salary, I'd never sell another policy unless I had to. The way things look, I'll be driving to Omaha in two weeks."

"I'm sorry—"

"Oh, it's not too bad. It has some great benefits. But what about this press conference? It may be your chance to set the record straight."

"I don't know," Leaner said. "But if I don't show up, that would be taken the wrong way too."

"Right. And you can bet Catalina will have Buck Hollingsworth there. Catalina has him in his back pocket. Look, just play your golf, collect your winnings and take off. If nothing else, you've had a good time with Catalina's granddaughter. She's a real knockout."

"She's mad as a hatter."

"She's also coming this way," Sherman said, pointing outside.

Leaner went to the window. "Stay here in the cabin while she's here, Sherman," he said, monitoring Margot's approach. "She might take it easy in front of company."

Margot hesitated a moment on the porch. Leaner returned casually to his chair to drink his beer. Sherman was looking through the curtains. "You want me to let her in?"

"Let 'er in."

Sherman threw open the door. Margot stood in the doorway, eyeing them. "And what are you two up to?"

"Having a few beers," Leaner said.

"Care to join us?" Sherman asked.

"No, no, thank you very much indeed, but I don't wish to burden Mister Leaner. I know he has a million things on his mind. I have a message for you," she went on.

"I thought that was one of Fenner's chores."

"Uncle Leo is busy setting up the press conference. Besides, Granddaddy didn't ask me to come over here. He has a list of names posted of the players to be interviewed, and your name's at the top of the list."

"I figured that."

"The thing is," Margot said, "that the press conference might be just like the canoe racing and the Scrabble playing. It could fall in the category of your contract for unnamed or to-be-named activities."

"So he could keep me from finishing the tournament if I don't show up...."

"I'm not sure," she said, "but he has three lawyers on the payroll."

"You'd better go," Sherman now advised him. "The important thing is to finish playing."

"He's right," Margot said. "Well, I'll be going."

Leaner got up and walked her to the door. He was moved that she had come to warn him, hardly could restrain himself from putting an arm around her shoulder. "Thank you," he said on the porch.

"You want a head job before I leave?"

"I guess not," Leaner said. In truth, he would have loved one but felt a need to hack away at some of the complications that clung to him like crawling vines. Besides, self-denial created the illusion that he controlled the events of his life rather than the other way around.

Sherman and Leaner were into the second six-pack by the time the press conference began. They quickly made for the club, where a banquet table had been set up on the stage. There were microphones and pitchers of ice water and nameplates in front of various chairs. It looked like the setting for a high school debate. Leaner climbed up and took his seat two down from Catalina, scanning the room for the reporter Randall and Buck Hollingsworth. Sherman gave him the thumbs-up sign and sat near the exit.

Fenner walked in and bent over Catalina, whispering something in his ear. Catalina covered his microphone with one hand, taking notes on a tablet with the other.

He stopped writing and cleared his throat while Fenner took a seat on the floor level.

"Ladies and gentlemen," Catalina announced, "as you know, Mister Buck Hollingsworth was to have been here, but I'm sorry to announce that he's come down with a rather painful pinched nerve just after finishing a fine round. He *will* be available to the press in the morning at the practice green, and of course at the first tee prior to the third round. Buck finished today with a sixty-eight, so he's anchored firmly in second place. As you all know, our second round leader is sitting to my left over here."

Leaner nodded to the room, feeling strange. Was this the wages of getting to be a name?

"So, should you have any questions of Mister Leaner or myself, or any of the other gentlemen on our panel of experts, fire away."

Leaner couldn't decide whether he felt more like a television panelist or a defendant at the Nuremburg trials.

There were only a few reporters, a dozen at most, and none appeared too anxious to begin the questioning. They were not exactly members of the sports-reporting establishment. *Golf Digest* was not represented. Nor was *Sports Illustrated*. In each case the writer had missed a deadline or somehow fouled up a story. Covering the Catalina Invitational was the journalistic equivalent of being sent to Siberia. They were like everything Leaner had begun to associate with the Catskills—a touch off-balance, and second-rate. Himself included.

One of them in the back raised a hand.

"I'd like to ask Mister Leaner a question. Most of the year's major tournaments have been played already. The Masters, the U.S., Canadian and British opens. Even the Houston Open, in your own home town. My question is, with the way you're playing, why are you just now starting on the tour, and why the Catalina Invitational?"

Leaner leaned over his microphone. "I had previous commitments," he said, then sat back in his chair.

"Could you elaborate on that?"

"No."

"What Mister Leaner means," Catalina butted in, "is that he leads a full and satisfying life in Houston, a fine city and a favorite of mine to visit. At any rate, his great love for golf not only qualified him as a pro but distinguished him enough for me to take notice when I scoured this year's ranks of rookies. I sent him an invitation and he was kind enough to comply. Next question."

Another reporter stood. "I watched a remarkable round of golf today, Mister Leaner. You're not a big man. Do you have some special technique for getting such long and accurate drives? And what about the putting? I've never seen so many one-putt greens in a single round."

Leaner's thumb rubbed his ear lobe. "It's nothing so special," he said. "You can learn the techniques from any good golf book—"

"Mister Leaner has a healthy respect for the game's fundamentals," Catalina broke in. "And he has a knack for managing his play, hole by hole. He's extremely talented and far too modest to admit it. The distance in his drives? Mister Leaner knows the importance of not only his arms, but his legs, shoulders, hips and feet for generating power. As for his putting, few of us are blessed with such a gift. As we sit here at the midway point of the Invitational, he has proven himself both accurate and, more importantly, consistent."

Leaner poured a glass of ice water. The press conference so far was a piece of cake. He was relieved that Catalina was out to grab all the limelight he could. Fine. It was Catalina's show, and it took the heat off him.

But another question suggested he'd been set up. "There's been some unfavorable reaction to your conduct, Mister Leaner. Some are saying that public figures, athletes, should be role models of behavior. I don't need to rehash what's been printed about you in the past several days. That's one side of the story. My question is, what do you have to say in defense of your outrageous behavior?"

"*Nothing*," Leaner said, and backed away from the mike.

"One of your fellow players said you hold both the fans and other golfers in contempt. How do you answer that?"

Leaner wondered who the hell would say that, then looked at Catalina, who began to speak when Leaner wouldn't, couldn't.

"Everyone says and does things during the heat of competition. Thurmond is young. While I don't condone certain behavior, I think you ought to keep things in perspective—"

"But that doesn't explain spitting at cameras."

"No, it doesn't," Catalina said, "but..."

Leaner took it as his cue. He stood up, pulling his

chair out from the table and picking up his nameplate.

"This entire salivary incident," Catalina was saying, "is the result of an accidental loss of control due to an allergy."

Leaner now figured that if Catalina was to speak for him, he should use his name as well, and placed the nameplate in front of Catalina's. He stepped down from the stage and aimed for the exit.

"I am reminded of an old expression my mother favored," Catalina said, not missing a beat. "She was in the habit of saying, 'Maxwell, don't make a mountain out of a molehill.' Have you gentlemen of the press ever heard that phrase before? Don't make mountains out of molehills, boys. That's what my mother was in the habit of saying when exaggeration got the better of me."

By this time, Leaner had left the building, not wanting to admit to himself that maybe Maxwell was a horse's ass but he sure had helped him up there. Who the hell did he think he was?

15

HE WAS AWAKE HALF
the night from the excitement over his commanding
lead in the tournament. He was hungry but couldn't
eat more than half a sandwich. As he lay in bed he was
expecting Margot to waltz through his cabin door.
Maybe she had given up on him, taken him at his
discouraging word. And now that he didn't have her,
he wanted her. She was a part of the Catskills to him
by now, and it wasn't the same without her. He really
owed her for tipping him off about his loss if he boy-
cotted the press conference. Still, he couldn't very well
call Catalina's house and ask her to come on over. There
would be plenty of explaining to do if he pulled a stunt
like that. It wasn't easy, though. The sheets were still
scented lightly with her fragrance of sandalwood.

He was pulling his shirt over his head when he felt
a sneeze coming on. He hesitated, elbows aimed skyward, holding his breath. It was a tug of war for a few
seconds, and the sneeze not only gave in, but Leaner's
sinuses cleared entirely, his congestion receding like a

175

wave ebbing out to sea. He would not, he felt, sneeze all day.

He finished dressing and was walking toward the first tee when he realized he was being booed. He had no idea how his walkout from yesterday's press conference had been handled by the papers, but he saw a connection. A moon-faced boy struggling with puberty blocked his path, hands cupped about his mouth. "Boo!" the boy hooted in a cracking adolescent voice. "You're a bum, Leaner. Boo!"

"You want to knock that off?" Leaner said as he passed him.

The boy made no attempt to follow him, but Leaner could hear his catcalls long after he disappeared from view. Leaner figured that the boy had read something about him in the papers. He decided, though, that keeping up with his public image, already tarnished, would put a strain on his game. Plenty of time after the tournament for that sort of thing.

The crowd was becoming so dense he had difficulty finding his way to the tee. He couldn't believe such a large overnight increase in attendance. Catalina should be happy. He had to squeeze sideways just to get through. He met Sherman head-on coming toward him.

"Where did they all come from?" Leaner asked him.

"Catalina roped off the grandstand area. You can hardly get to the first tee. Follow me around this way."

"The gallery won't be able to see anything," Leaner said, letting Sherman lead him out the back way.

"Sure they can," Sherman said. "All they need is a periscope. Fenner's selling them."

"Oh, sure. I forgot the periscopes."

"Did you see today's papers?"

"I don't want to. I just got booed."

"That's tough," Sherman said. They were taking an extremely long route to the course.

"Of course it was just one kid. I mean, think about a quarterback with a stadium full of people doing it... why are we going this way?"

"Because where we were funnels down to nothing and there's no way to move. I heard that the periscope business was slow until Catalina corraled the gallery."

"I'd sure hate for him to get stuck with extra periscopes." They smiled at each other.

"I looked at one of them," Sherman said. "They're all cardboard except the mirrors are glass. Turn this way. Head for that tree."

"He's making almost seven bucks on each one he sells."

"He's a smart old geezer, all right," Sherman said. "Where in the hell are we?"

"I thought you'd already been this way."

"No, it just looked less crowded in this direction."

"Maybe we ought to go back."

"I think we're near the caddies' barracks," Sherman said. "Yeah, I'm sure that's where we are. So the course sort of surrounds us from here."

"The course is four miles long," Leaner reminded him.

They walked among some trees that looked to Leaner like a neglected orchard—there was symmetry to their layout. They looked down each row of trees as they walked on, and at the end of one of the rows they saw a wooden building, its paint peeling.

"There it is." Sherman pointed. "You know the story behind the barracks, don't you?"

"No."

"It was Catalina's home until the tournament got him on his feet. He won it in a crap game just before getting out of the army. I heard he had fifteen or twenty Jeeps and a bazooka thrown in with it."

"We're lucky he didn't make us play World War Two after the Scrabble."

"Next time ... let's head over there and commandeer us a golf cart," Sherman said.

There was an older man puttering about in front of the barracks. He was in charge of the caddies, making sure they were assigned and doing their work. He was sweeping the wooden steps when Leaner and Sherman approached.

"I know you"—the old man pointed—"you're that Leaner fellow, ain't you?"

"That's right," Leaner said, "and we're supposed to tee off in a few minutes. I don't suppose you could run us over to the first tee, could you?"

"It would be my honor," the overseer said. "But if we happen to run into Mister Catalina, you'll tell him that you fellows asked me to bring you over, won't you? He doesn't like me to wander too far from the barracks. . . . Well, I'll be doggone, I got Leaner right here on my doorstep."

He disappeared. A minute later he met them in front of the barracks in an electric cart. He drove them along a dirt path through acres of shade. When he let them out, he said his name was John.

"Thanks for the ride, John," Leaner said, shaking his hand.

"Doggone," old John said, and zipped away in the cart.

The periscopes in the vicinity of the first tee had turned the gallery into a sea of peeping toms. No one really was able to see all that much better with a periscope, but when you paid nine bucks you had to believe.

Ray Reasoner and the threesome's caddies were waiting for Leaner and Sherman. "Where have you two monkeys been?" Reasoner asked Leaner.

"You know how it is," Leaner told him, deciding to take a shot in the dark. "Holding golfers and fans in contempt can be a full-time job."

"What? I was assured my name wouldn't be used," he muttered more loudly than he wanted as he turned away.

"It wasn't," Leaner said, after Sherman made his tee shot. He selected his driver as Jonah held the bag before him like a *sommelier* presenting a patron with a fine wine.

"Jonah, you're doing one hell of a job," Leaner said. "I've got to hand it to you. For someone with your background, that is, zero experience, I've no complaints. Are they feeding you all right in the barracks?"

Jonah smiled. "Mr. John is a good cook," was all he said.

Reasoner had made his drive, and Leaner teed up, still chatting with his caddy. "He's a likable old-timer," he said, wondering what had possessed him to use that particular term. He was certain he would resent it if someone called him that when he was an old-timer himself. "John seems a little more down-home than most of the northerners I've met so far—"

"Take your damn shot," someone in the gallery yelled. Leaner waved in that general direction.

"I'll talk with John for you if you like," Leaner went on. "Today's Saturday, and you'll be out of a job tomorrow evening. John may be able to hire you on."

"I do not know," Jonah said.

"Give it some thought," Leaner told him, then took his time, squared himself with the ball and began his third round with a shot that ended up, with a roll, nearly three hundred yards away on the edge of the fairway. The applause was strangely muffled, but Leaner turned and faced the gallery's acknowledgement. Periscopes bobbed up and down everywhere while their owners clapped their hands.

Leaner withdrew into himself again, determined to press his game as he had in the second round. He figured if he made par or close to it for the third round, Catalina could start filling his name in on the first-place check, like Sherman said....

But something was happening today that wasn't in the script. Good shots were offset by subsequent misfortunes. Putts that would have dropped on Friday pulled up a foot short today, or hung on the lip, or rimmed the cup. Chip shots had too little or too much underspin. Purposeful slices and hooks either went too far or stayed on line when they weren't supposed to. He hovered near par the entire day—one up, even, one down, even again. His play was adequate, but nothing like the firestorm of a game his two previous rounds had been. Still, he had built up a ten-stroke lead in those rounds, and average decent play was still all he would need for victory, and that was what he had going so far.

Victory. For Leaner, the word went hand in hand with pain and bleeding. Victory was something reserved for

wars or boxing. It only now occurred to him that there
was a cleaner, sweeter taste to the word. He had beaten
a lot of people at golf over the years, but to have it in
his grasp when it counted, playing for real money, that
was very much something else. Even the fans looked
different to him. They seemed to appreciate his talent,
his ability to control the game they loved yet could
never approach in the way he could. He had the touch.

Leaner noticed that Ray Reasoner had sliced a couple
of his drives back-to-back, and on the tenth hole he
stood behind him to look at his swing, having forgiven
the man his bad-mouthing. After all, Leaner was on
his way to winning his first pro tournament. He could
afford to be a little magnanimous. Reasoner sliced again,
and Leaner offered a suggestion.

"I think your club face is a little out of line—"

"I think *you're* a little out of line."

Leaner pushed on. "It's something small, you probably can't see it yourself—"

"Show me on the next hole," Reasoner said, relent-
ing a little. "Hey, if my lab was on fire and I could run
in and save only one instrument, you know which one
it would be?"

"No," Leaner said, dumbfounded at this response to
a slice.

"My barometer," Reasoner told him, first and foremost a weatherman.

Leaner teed up now on Number Ten. It was a bugger,
a 460-yard par four with the green obscured because of
a gentle curving of the fairway to the left. Sand traps
lined the entire fairway, and if you didn't play it just
right you were almost surely in a bunker.

Leaner's drive was a touch too strong and off-direction, and the ball plopped into the sand where the fairway bent to the left. Most of the players couldn't even reach that far, so this time Leaner's distance worked against him. He had to blast out from a bad lie, but hit a lovely five iron four feet from the pin and sank his putt for another par. It could have been a birdie.

The whole day went like that. He did manage to get a birdie on Eighteen, like a fisherman hanging a little bass on his last cast of the day.

After they finished the round Sherman said to him, "I just heard Hollingsworth had an eight on Fourteen. He's dropped to fourth place."

"How could you hear that? I've been with you all along and I didn't hear it."

"Someone in the gallery whispered it while you were putting out. It just happened."

"Jesus, you get your information fast," Leaner said, offering his putter to Jonah. "Have you made up your mind yet?" he asked him. Jonah hadn't the faintest idea what Leaner was referring to. He suffered from an abundance of drugs unfamiliar to his system, plus a lack of sleep. Life in the caddies' barracks was rowdy.

"I do not know."

Jonah's persistent refusal to use contractions in his speech suddenly irritated Leaner. "You don't have much time," he said. "I'll speak to John if you'd like. If you'd rather I didn't, fine."

"Yes," Jonah said, catching the drift of the conversation at last. "Speak to Mister John for me, if you will."

* * *

Leaner cleaned up and was lounging in the cabin when he decided to talk to old John in the barracks on behalf of Jonah. It was quite a walk over there and he didn't feel like going out. He picked up the phone and called the switchboard.

"Put me through to the caddies' barracks."

"What business do you have there?"

"Goddammit...Fenner, is that you?"

"Yes, it's me. What do you want with the caddies?"

"I'm going to round them up for a serenade beneath Catalina's window, if you must know."

Leaner's answer was taken on its face by poor Fenner. The call was connected, and Leaner identified himself to John.

"Why would the likes of you be ringing me up?" John wanted to know.

"It's about my caddy, Jonah. He and I are parting company tomorrow and I was wondering if there was a place for him here with you."

"We're not open year-round up here, you know. It's not like Texas. We get snowed in up here."

"I can well imagine," Leaner said. "What are Jonah's chances of working the season as a caddy?"

"I wouldn't know. Mister Catalina does all the hiring and firing. . . . Say, I believe you're gonna win the show this year, you lucky dog, you."

"Thanks for your confidence, John."

"You rascal," John added.

"Thank you, John," Leaner said, and hung up before John could hang any more crusty endearments on him. Besides, praise had a tendency to embarrass him. He lifted the phone again.

"What do you want now?" Fenner asked.

"Let me talk to Catalina."

"Are the caddies willing?"

"Yes," Leaner said. "Let's keep it our secret, though. We'll make it a surprise."

"Max will be touched," Fenner said, transferring the call to Catalina.

"Max Catalina."

"Mister Catalina, this is Thurmond Leaner."

"Yes, Thurmond, I recognize your voice. How may I help you?"

"My caddy needs more employment than I can give him. Would you be willing to take him on as a regular caddy? He's very good."

"I'm rather busy at the moment," Catalina said. "Can we discuss it in the morning, say at nine? You don't tee off until ten, and I wanted to go over a few things with you anyway."

"Fine," Leaner said.

"I've scheduled a post-tourney press conference during which I'll present you with a check for your winnings. I hope you'll not abandon us this time."

"I'll be there," Leaner said.

He hung up, thinking that it really would be over in less than a day. He would receive a paycheck for his work, and be on his way—to Boston, he had decided.

He saw Margot walking toward the cabin and realized that she, like Jonah, would soon be a part of his Catskillian past. He went out to the porch and welcomed her, comfortably wrapping himself around her. "Hello, Brown Eyes," and she melted in his arms.

The sun went down. They had dinner in the club. They filled up on lobster and wine. A tourist approached once and asked for Leaner's autograph. He signed the woman's menu. She thanked him, and remarked that his young wife was lovely. Leaner immediately purchased a second bottle of wine, which they chilled in the cabin.

Leaner still couldn't sleep from the exhilaration of all the recent events. He wasn't apprehensive or full of nerves. He was driven by excitement, the promise of the future. Who could sleep? Margot's mood took a turn for the frisky, so it fitted right in that he wasn't a sleepyhead. Intertwined, they finally dropped off. What a life I'm having, Leaner thought before closing his eyes.

16

LEANER HAD DISTINGUISHED
himself as a golfer, as a home remodeler, as a traveler,
as a Texan, as both employer and employee, and as a
lover. He was also thought of as a bum, a spitter, a
lucky dog and a rascal. But foremost on this, his fourth
and final day in the tournament, the component which
would most greatly influence his entire venture to the
Catskills was that part of him that was a sneezer. His
name might as well have been Sneezer, for within him,
while he tied his golf shoes that morning, was the
Grandfather Sneeze, the one that had almost surfaced
the previous day. The sneeze had built strength like a
hurricane over water, and Leaner could scarcely prepare
for it before it erupted. He recoiled from it as if he had
been shot, and then a series of aftersneezes threw him
violently forward. He sounded like a volley of howit-
zers. Rather than the pleasant sense of relief one nor-
mally feels after a sneeze, Leaner felt something wrong,
and a moment later a sharp throbbing along his spine
caused him to drop the shoelace.

Leaner's back was frozen.

The commotion had stirred Margot. "What is it?" she asked sleepily. She had been dreaming that there was an earthquake while Leaner was sneezing.

"Something bad," he said. "I don't think I can move."

Margot had never heard of anyone waking up paralyzed, and thought that Leaner was pulling an impromptu lover's ruse. She scooted across the bed to his side and began to pat his back as softly as if she were burping a baby. "My poor man," she said in mock sympathy.

The pain sprung Leaner from the bed. He landed on his feet, but his posture was that of a question mark. "I screwed up my back!" he yelled. He tried to bend over again, but the pain told him to stop. "I had it made, I was in the driver's seat. One sneeze and I'm under the gun."

"You're not kidding, are you?"

He glared at her.

"Maybe if you tried to lie down it would straighten you out again."

Leaner did just that. It was all he could do to bear the pain, and gritting his teeth didn't help. In stages, like unfolding a ladder, he stretched onto the bed and observed Margot at his feet, tying his other shoe. She was still naked.

"There," she said after making the bow, "feel better?"

"I'm dying," he said.

The telephone rang. Leaner reached for the receiver and heard sobbing on the other end of the line.

"Who is it?"

"Oh, Thurmond, it's terrible."

"Lauren, what is it? What's the matter?"

"It's Bingo," she cried. "I had him out in the backyard yesterday for his drills and his leash just snapped. He scampered up a tree and disappeared over the rooftop. I haven't seen him since. I've put signs up all over the neighborhood."

"I can't render an opinion right now," Leaner said. "I feel like I've broken my back, and I have to figure out what to do about it. I'll call you soon. Goodbye." And he hung up.

"That was her, wasn't it?" Margot said.

"Give me a break, Margot. What can I say to you? That I don't love her anymore? That I want you to come with me when I leave? It isn't the truth. You're a loving person, Margot, but—"

"I've loved you from the moment I saw you. And that's the truth, too."

He sighed. "Will you help me up? I have a meeting with your grandfather."

Margot again dutifully folded and unfolded Leaner, and was about to allow him to baby-step out the door. ...Instead she flew across the floor and wrapped her arms around one of his legs. "Don't leave me!"

Leaner looked to the heavens. He felt himself at once the victim and perpetrator. Actually, he knew he had only himself to blame for his predicament. He was allergic to Margot's deodorant, which contained mangos. What he said aloud was a muttered, "Undone by mangos, for God's sake."

She thought the words were peculiar and released her hold on him, as if Leaner had broken a spell. He then trudged out the door, his back stooping him as if he were walking in a blizzard.

On the way to Catalina's office he studied his shadow, noticing how effortlessly it glided while his body was such an unwieldy piece of freight to move. He didn't know what had happened in his back, and only hoped that the vertebrae wouldn't fuse into a solid pipe. He took the stairs in the club one at a time, resting on each step and leading with same foot like an arthritic old man. He paced himself in the corridor to avoid compounding his injury and finally made it into the office. Seeing that Catalina was out, he fell back into one of the stuffed chairs, closing his eyes until he heard footsteps. He gripped the armrests as a pacifier.

"I told you my door was always open," Catalina announced, seating himself behind his desk. "Didn't I say that?"

Leaner nodded.

"Now, what's this you wanted to see me about?"

"My back—"

"No, it wasn't your back. Give me a minute. It wasn't the press conference. I already covered that. It certainly couldn't be too dark to play again."

"Mister Catalina," Leaner said. "Something happened to me. I had a bad sneeze and my back got hurt. I can hardly walk and I don't know how I'll play. Even if I can, I'll slow down our threesome—"

Catalina clapped his hands. "That's it! There's some uncovered ground. You're not a threesome today. Buck Hollingsworth is joining your group. You're a full-fledged foursome again. How's that for giving the gallery what they want? The leader and the name, slugging it out toe to toe."

"I may not even be able to play. Aren't you listening?"

Catalina studied him from behind his desk. "A pinched nerve," he diagnosed. "Stand up. Let me give you the old Catalina back-snapper."

Leaner raised his hand in the manner of a policeman halting traffic. "There's no way in hell you're touching my back," he said.

Catalina jumped up from his chair and stood in front of Leaner. "I'll go get Leo," he threatened. "The two of us will hold you down if we have to. You want to be stubborn? You're talking with Mister Stubborn. Stand up now. It's for your own benefit."

Leaner couldn't have stood if his chair had been a catapult. He shook his head, and Catalina walked out of the room.

"Leo!" Leaner heard him call. "Front and center, on the double!" He *felt* Fenner's footsteps as he stomped up the stairs. Catalina whispered something to his brother-in-law in the doorway and the two of them moved to either side of Leaner's chair, each man gripping him beneath an armpit.

"Oh, you bastards," Leaner moaned while being lifted. "God, that *hurts....*"

"That's the pain talking, Leo," Catalina said. "Pay him no mind."

"The pain, hell," Leaner said as they maneuvered him. "You two have been itching for the chance, and now you have it."

When they had him in the desired position, Catalina

stood in the chair Leaner had vacated and Fenner held Leaner's arms to his sides. Catalina then proceeded to land a volley of little rabbit punches between Leaner's shoulder blades.

"That ought to fix him up. You can let go of him, Leo."

"That's *it*?" Leaner said. "That's the Catalina back-snapper?"

"And don't you feel a world of difference?"

"*No*. You didn't do anything at all." He collected himself, taking three or four breaths. "My caddy," he said, "that's what I wanted to talk to you about. Will you hire him on for your club? I'm sure that just room and board in the barracks and a little allowance would keep him happy."

It was Catalina's turn now to be flabbergasted. "Hire your *caddy*?" he said, making the final word sound vile, as if he was saying, "Eat some *maggots*?" He stepped down from the chair and skulked to his desk. "Of all the presumptuous suggestions. I fix his back, Leo, and this is the thanks I get."

"What's so terrible about hiring my caddy?"

Catalina shuffled some papers, doing his best to ignore Leaner. Leaner didn't consider asking for a postponement because of his back. He made for the door. Fenner followed, and when they were outside he said, "When should I count on the serenade?"

"The what?"

"The caddy serenade."

"I couldn't manage it," Leaner said. "Sorry."

Fenner let him hobble away, his face showing disappointment. Leaner heard him mutter something under his breath.

Oh, God, what crazies. Maybe him included. After all, he was here too, wasn't he? He managed to push himself forward, each step warning him never again to take his back for granted. He wondered if he would end up wearing a brace or, worse, be saddled with a walker by the time he was thirty.

He wondered, too, if he could swing a golf club.

Jonah had his clubs, so with a half-hour remaining before tee-off, he went to Sherman's cabin. When Sherman opened the door, his face dropped at the sight of his neighbor.

"My God, what happened to you?"

"I threw out my back with a sneeze. Can I borrow a club? I have to see if I can still swing one."

Sherman handed him a five iron and they went outside. Leaner let the club rest in his hands. He gritted his teeth, tightening his grip. He winced in the backswing, unwound and followed through. As the club made its whooshing sound he felt he was being thrown backward against a brick wall.

"How did it look?"

"To tell the truth," Sherman said, "like you were chopping down a tree."

"What am I going to do?"

"Play conservatively," Sherman said. "With the lead you have on the field you can still salvage a decent overall score. Hell, even a bogey on every hole would put you only nine or so over par for the tournament."

"Don't say that," Leaner said, returning the club.

"I'm not saying that's going to happen," Sherman said. "I'm sure you'll at least shoot under ninety."

Depressed, Leaner returned to his own cabin to formulate a strategy. Clearly, he would have to compensate for his back. He felt if he maintained distance in his shots, then the path of the ball might corkscrew out of control. And if he concentrated on the direction his ball took, he was certain that distance would be sacrificed.

Margot walked out of the bathroom, while he sat ruminating on the couch, and nearly scared him to death. That was something the women in his life had in common. They all walked quietly and startled him with their abrupt presence. He shook his head.

"What kind of a man would allow his own grand-daughter to shack up for days on end with a professional golfer?" he asked her.

She was leaning forward, bent at the waist, vigor-ously brushing her hair. "He's busy," she said between strokes. "When I came to visit for the summer he told me that the week of the tournament I was on my own. He said his hands would be full, and from what I've seen, they are." She stood straight again, her face flushed. Leaner enviously wished that his back was in good enough condition to bend and twist like that.

"Are you going to watch me today?"

"Sure," she said. "I'm rooting for my man."

"I'm not your man." It was an automatic response.

"You don't need to say that. I've seen the way you look at me when you don't think I see you. Like I'm nutty or something." She smiled then. "But you are my man for the rest of the day."

Margot was a great help in getting him to the first tee in time. The pain he held captive in his back was duller now, but there was no getting around it. He walked funny, and some of the gallery laughed at the sight of him, thinking he was clowning around to ease the tension of the tournament.

Actually he was a little early. Sherman had already clued in Reasoner about Leaner's injury, suggesting that neither of them clap him on the back if he was to be congratulated.

Catalina, or rather Catalina's market research team, had been right about increasing the crowd size by teaming Leaner and Buck Hollingsworth. The gallery was huge.

Leaner didn't see Jonah anywhere, and hoped that Catalina hadn't banned him from the course out of vindictiveness. He saw Sherman's and Reasoner's caddies, and a third he assumed was Hollingsworth's. Finally, he asked Sherman if he'd seen Jonah.

"He's right over there." Sherman pointed.

Leaner looked. "I don't see him."

"With the other two caddies. He's changed clothes."

Leaner at last saw him. Jonah had indeed discarded his heavy woolen attire, replacing it with a loud Hawaiian print shirt tied at the stomach, baggy white drawstring pants, cork platform sandals, a Panama hat and canary-yellow framed sunglasses.

"Good Lord," Leaner said. "I've created a monster. He looks like Mick Jagger."

There was a disturbance behind them, and Leaner turned to see the gallery parting to allow someone through. Catalina's car horn was honking in the middle of the activity, and every periscope in view was tilted in that direction. It was Leaner's first sighting of him, and until that moment he had doubted that Buck Hollingsworth was even at the Catalina. He had cer-

tainly hoped he was not, because in spite of his asser-
tions to the contrary, playing against Buck
Hollingsworth was not his idea of a no-pressure golfing
debut, chopping down trees with other no-names like
himself.

And now he had a crippling bad back, too.

17

LEANER REALIZED HE HAD
to get out of his negative frame of mind. He had to
remember that his twelve-stroke lead gave him plenty
of leeway to work out a game plan that took into account the diminished capacity of his back. It was time
to pull in on the reins of his charging-rhino approach
to the course and play as if he were on a tightrope. He
would need to barricade his game from assault, forming
a last line of defense against anyone who tried to take
him.

By the cheering of the gallery at Buck Hollingsworth's arrival, one would have thought he had already
clinched the tournament and been knighted Lord of
the Catskills as well. "'Atta boy, Buck!" and "Go get
'em Buck" and other hearty first-name enthusiasms
pelted the air about him. Hollingsworth could cause
near pandemonium with a simple wave of the hand,
with the crowd swarming around him. Leaner's isolated fans, when they greeted his stoop-shouldered ap-

pearance, sounded like aged professors calling roll in a
class they weren't fond of teaching.

Leaner watched the group pile out of Catalina's little
amphibious car. Hollingsworth and Catalina were
jammed into the front seat; Fenner was squeezed into
the back with his boy Joey, also Hollingsworth's caddy.
The entourage wormed through the crowd to the tee,
and Hollingsworth immediately greeted his new playing partners, reaching Leaner last.

"Missed you at the PGA last week." He grinned,
pumping Leaner's hand.

"I had a family reunion I had to go to," Leaner said.

"The way you've been playing, lucky for us you
couldn't make it."

"I hurt my back this morning," Leaner said.

Hollingsworth looked sharply at him, smelling an
advance cop-out. He turned away and headed for his
clubs.

Catalina had hold of his bullhorn again, preparing to
give this starring foursome a big send-off. "Ladies and
gentlemen, my personal thanks for making this the
largest and most successful Max Catalina Invitational
Golf Tournament to date. Our attendance today is nearly
fourteen thousand. I know you join me in pulling for
your favorites. The beauty of the game is never knowing the winner until the last putt drops. But keep an
eye on this group we have here. Because I have the
sneaking suspicion that one of them will walk away
with a trophy, and a check for thirty thousand dollars.
Am I right, Buck? Do you concur, Thurmond?"

The gallery burst into applause the length of the
546-yard first hole. Leaner wished he had the bullhorn

for a few moments to warn the crowd not to expect miracles from him, that his back had had, so to speak, the rug pulled out from under it by a sneeze. He averted his eyes from the crowd. Jonah approached him, presenting him his club.

"Did you see my new clothing?" he asked proudly.

"A blind man could see those clothes," Leaner told him. When he saw that the words had stung his caddy, he added, "But they look fine, really fine."

He took his club from Jonah, wondering what would become of him after the tournament. Surely he must have spent all his earnings on his new clothes. If he hadn't, he couldn't have much left. Since Catalina had refused to discuss his employment, Leaner assumed that Jonah would be on the road again. He pulled his caddy aside and pressed another fifty dollars in his hand. Jonah accepted the gratuity, and Leaner felt that his obligation to the youngster had reasonably ended. Henceforth, Jonah would have to get by in the world without his patronage. Now it was time for Leaner to try to hold onto his golf game. He felt like a scaled-down version of himself and said as much to Jonah while awaiting his turn at the tee. "This isn't the real me today," he said.

Sherman and Reasoner had hit solid drives. Buck Hollingsworth followed, and although his shot wasn't as well placed as Sherman's, Hollingsworth's loyal subjects went bananas. A few broken periscopes even sailed high into the air like midshipmen's caps at graduation. Leaner hoped that the crowd was only experiencing the excitement of the opening of the final round, that maybe the giddiness was temporary. He badly wanted the gallery to settle down, but of course there was no way to address the crowd and recommend such a thing. He was sure that if he stepped the slightest bit out of line with the fans they would turn on him in a minute, transformed into a haranguing little-league infield, hurling nerve-shattering verbal assaults.... "Hey, Leaner, putter can't putt, putter can't putt...." Because of his back, Leaner felt a jittery tension. If he could somehow transfer those jitters down his club shafts and into his game, he might be okay. But the crowd... Not that he didn't appreciate some fans rooting for him. If only he could huddle with them and appoint them crowd-control monitors, he could put the noise out of his mind and maybe settle down to his game.

To spare his back, Leaner had Jonah tee up the ball for him. This action, interpreted as laziness among the Hollingsworth faction of the gallery, spawned boos. Leaner did his best to concentrate. He gripped the club firmly as he could, double-checking the heel and toe of the club to be absolutely certain he was sticking to the basics. Regardless of what remained of his swing, he at least wanted the club face to meet the ball head-on. He would try compensating for his back by allowing his arms and legs to assume some of the extra load.

He swung. The pain was excruciating during the follow-through, and as he searched the air for his ball, the gallery gasped in disbelief.

Leaner had missed the ball entirely. He'd *fanned*, for God's sake.

He quickly pretended that it was a practice swing, smiled to reassure them. Repeating the procedure, the pain shot into his back once more. His spinal column was on fire. This time the ball flew toward its target.

He had sliced and it was short, but at least he had managed to avoid the rough.

"There you go," Hollingsworth cheered Leaner, walking by his side down the fairway. "Tell me something. Did you fellas really let Max talk you into racing canoes to qualify?"

"We had no choice," Leaner said. "Two guys got cut that way."

Hollingsworth guffawed. "He told me," he said, wiping his eyes after a hearty laugh. "I just didn't know whether to believe him. He's such a character."

The foursome hit second shots. Leaner wanted to cry every time he raised his arms, but had convinced himself that while it was painful he was doing himself no lasting harm. He was young, heretofore healthy, and could rehabilitate. He had never had one, but he suspected that his back was having a muscle spasm. He could feel twinges every now and then where the entire strap of muscles along one side would clench and knot itself. The muscles were playing tug-of-war with each other to such an extent that they were pulling his spine out of its vertical plane, like wringing out a wet washcloth. No doubt that was why it hurt so much, but the vision of thirty thousand dollars was a powerful anesthetic.

He saw Catalina following the progress of the foursome in his convertible, driving right in the fairway to avoid the massive gallery. Margot had joined her grandfather in the car, and Fenner was loping alongside like a Secret Service man. Leaner had to laugh at the sight of it in spite of his pain.

"I'd love to have seen those canoes," Hollingsworth was saying. "But I had to fly to New York and shoot a couple of spots for Kodak. I made it back just in time."

"Let's stop talking about the canoes," Leaner suggested.

Before choosing a club, Leaner always liked to picture how the shot should be. In his model, he could see the ball as it flew, could predict its behavior when it touched down. In theory, the closer he came to executing this ideal shot, the better his performance would be. With his back the way it was, he fell farther and farther from his thought-model. His third shot on the first hole illustrated this. Ninety yards out from the pin, Leaner used a nine iron. He had every reason to expect a high, arcing shot with enough backspin to brake the ball close to where it made its landing. But he was off. He topped the ball and it careened off the far end of the green, bouncing out of view somewhere in the woods. Which left him two shots from the depths of the rough to make par.

"That was unfortunate," Hollingsworth said.

"Right," Leaner answered, wanting to bury his nine iron in the man's skull.

"I heard you guys played Scrabble—"

"That's *right*," Leaner said, "and we had a real good time."

Leaner split off from him once more. There were so many people crowded near the green that he only had to look for an open spot in the crowd to locate his ball. He studied the shot. The gallery was pressed close. It was the farthest he had strayed from the fairway the whole tournament. He was really hemmed in, and the path they allowed for his projected chip was a narrow one.

He hit onto the green, temporarily feeling that he

might make par. But he'd underestimated his back's role in such a shot. It took two more strokes to get down. A bogey six. Hollingsworth, tied for second in the tournament, birdied the hole, cutting Leaner's lead to nine with seventeen to go. Leaner had Jonah retrieve his ball from the cup.

Sherman huddled with Leaner at the next tee. "You can't give up two strokes on every hole."

"No kidding."

"We're going to beat Hollingsworth, the bastard. I've been studying you. Would you like me to try coaching you the rest of the round?"

"You've got your own game to worry about—"

"That's okay, just listen. On the first hole you were slicing some, I think because you're overusing your legs. Doesn't give your hips time to unwind, your arms can't swing free."

"That's a little confusing."

"*Less legs*," Sherman said. "I know your back hurts, but less legs."

"I'll try. How come you're doing this for me?"

"Because I can't win and you still have a shot at it. Also, it was just like I suspected all along. Hollingsworth told me Catalina's promised him ten percent of the works, from pro shop sales to cups of beer."

"He can't lose, can he?" Leaner said.

"Yeah, a real sweetheart deal..."

The second hole was the par-four, 384-yard straight-away. Keeping Sherman's leg tip in mind, Leaner took what he felt was his natural swing. His back stung him again, and the ball hooked badly.

"What happened?" he asked Sherman.

"Not enough legs. Too much legs, you slice. Not

enough, you hook. Find the middle ground, adjust."

"This is damn frustrating," Leaner said, and walked off to the rough for his next shot. The ball, fortunately, had landed in a patch of moss and was above the surrounding vegetation as if it were sitting on a tee. Leaner was grateful. It was as though the Catskills themselves had suddenly pitched in to do their part in seeing him through this. With an open shot at the green, he took his six iron from Jonah with confidence, having imagined the ball not merely landing on the green but going right in the hole.

None of which, of course, happened. He had just as much trouble with his back as on the previous hole. Because it was a straight hole, he had pretty much taken it for granted, even with his back. Now he felt as if the hole was out to get him. He told himself he still had all his talent *somewhere* inside him, but he felt like a gold prospector piddling around with flakes, knowing that the mother lode was close by but just out of reach. He worried that his shots would disintegrate into wild ricochets. He was far short of the green with his six iron, and Hollingsworth had come up to him again. Just the medicine he needed.

"I think it was old Ben Hogan," Hollingsworth pointed out, "who said it's not how many good shots you make that win at golf, but how few bad ones."

"May I call you Buck?" Leaner said, lips tight.

"Sure thing."

"Well, Buck, I think you need to retire to a neutral corner. I don't know why you feel it necessary to bait me, but it's time to stop. What do you say?"

Hollingsworth snorted. "I don't have to use gamesmanship to beat the likes of a Thurmond Leaner," he said. "I can guarantee you *that.*"

"I've come to expect a lot of second-rate stuff up here," Leaner said, "but you're the biggest surprise of all, Buck. You really are." And moved away, hoping he'd made Buck back off a little.

The third hole was a slightly shorter par four than the last one. The fairway curved gently to the left, but at the place on the curve where the tee shot should land, it was surrounded by four sand traps. A slice, a hook or a ball hit too far could put you on the beach. Like most golf courses, Catalina's seemed to have been designed by a sadist.

At the tee Sherman squeezed Leaner's arm. "Remember what I said about legs."

"I *know* about legs. I know about arms and hips too, but I seem to be falling apart and I can't do anything about it."

"Then let's fall apart *gradually*," Sherman said. "Remember, you're *winning* this tournament right at this very moment. Now go up there and put the ball nice and easy between those bunkers."

It was no Knute Rockne speech but there was a firmness to Sherman's voice that Leaner had not heard before and it did lift his spirits. He addressed the ball and, forcing himself to disregard his back pains, drove it straight down the middle. Which wasn't the idea on this hole—one needed to draw it slightly to the left. The gallery, seeing the ball was headed for a bunker, gasped and shouted like eyewitnesses to an imminent collision as the ball neared the sand. It seemed that as

Leaner's game deteriorated, he was winning some new support as the underdog.

The ball splashed into the sand some two hundred yards from the tee...and if the bunker had not been there, the ball clearly would have bounced off into the woods. Which was what Sherman quickly pointed out to him. It could have been much worse. "Don't look back," he said. "Play what's ahead of you, don't think about mistakes."

Leaner nodded, took the advice to heart. Maybe too much. His next shot went from one trap to the other, and could not be blamed on his back. It was lack of concentration, and Leaner realized he was lucky to have moved the ball at all. Shaken, he pushed through the sand for another crack at it.

"You can't afford to give away shots like that," Sherman said.

Leaner ignored him. The next shot was just to get out of the sand, but he lay there, 140 yards from the pin on a par four. There was another bunker in front of the green, and Leaner's seven iron fell just shy of it. From there he wedged to within four feet of the pin and sank the putt. Still, it was a double bogey, and Hollingsworth had made another bird. Leaner's lead was down to six.

"Fifteen holes to go," Sherman reminded him. "We got that little par three ahead of us. You almost got a hole-in-one there, so you know what to do."

"I've known what to do on the first three holes too," Leaner told him. "My damn back won't let me do it."

Hollingsworth overheard the conversation. "A *professional* athlete wouldn't let something like that happen to his back."

"The ten-percenter is heard from," Leaner answered, and Hollingsworth, red-faced, moved off.

Leaner had directed a glance or two in Margot's direction during the round, and it wasn't like one of those old boxing movies where the hero is flat on the canvas and, seeing his girl at ringside, gets stoked with true grit, gets up and knocks out his opponent. Leaner, reaching for straws, thought of it nonetheless, seeing Cagney dismembering a guy against the ropes. For the first time he noticed that Margot had on one of his shirts, and that it looked great on her. She was leaning against the rear fender of Catalina's car, a light smile creasing her lips. She was nodding her head, which he interpreted as a gesture wishing him good luck. He wiggled the fingers of his right hand at her and she waved back.

He played the next four holes as if there was an earthquake in progress. Anyhow, that was how it seemed to him, and he half expected trees to uproot and fall in his path, and flame-belching chasms to open and char the atmosphere. On Five his ball rested in the mud bank of a pond. When he chipped to the nearby green there was an explosion of mud. One foot was soaked through to his sock, and some of the mud even managed to find its way behind one of his ears. On Six those tricky boulders jumped up and caught his drive in a head-on collision, bounced the ball right back to him. Seven, praise the Lord, he parred. But on Eight, a tough par three, he double-bogeyed. His game was steadily coming apart—the wheels were coming off, as the honey-toned TV-commentators liked to say. He hated all that fancy jargon. He did manage to move the ball, but in such uncertain fashion that he was grateful every time he sank a putt. With the clunk of the ball in the bottom of the cup he had at least overcome another obstacle, no matter how much over par he was.

Leaner had, in fact, now lost eleven strokes to Hollingsworth, who was having a great round. When Leaner bogeyed the Ninth, Hollingsworth moved in for a share of the lead with a routine par. The gallery loved it, not so much out of a dislike of Leaner; they just preferred a close head-to-head competition over someone running away with the tournament, leaving the rest of the field in his dust.

Before starting the back nine Leaner sat down on the close-cropped grass for a breather, a towel draped around his shoulders. His back throbbed. He was on the edge of a sinus infection. He tried to tell himself that he could be in worse shape, but he knew that he had better find some way to control his game, and fast. He lay his head back on the ground to straighten his spine and bent his knees a little to take the pressure off of it. He felt like crying, and in fact did a little into the towel, pretending at the same time to be wiping away his sweat.

18

LEANER HAD NOT KEPT
up with his own publicity. If he had, he would have
realized that, contrary to his expectations, the press
had rallied to his defense after his press conference.
They praised his golf and said he was right not to answer loaded questions. He was also the subject of two
editorials criticizing the slander of John Randall, who
had captured Leaner's sneeze on film and concocted
such lies about him. It was the photograph that had
gone out over the wires, but apparently its impact was
slight and transitory. Who, scanning a newspaper's fill-
ers over a cup of coffee, would see that oddity as anything but a hoax or maybe a publicity stunt if they
remembered it at all?

Who indeed? Jonah's father and grandfather, pan-
icked by what they were certain was the kidnapping
and corruption of their boy, were lamenting their loss
at a newsstand in Clarion, Pennsylvania, when the
photograph of Leaner and Jonah came to their attention. The grandfather, who recognized Leaner as the

man who had knocked Jonah out and sent X-rays through his head, loaded the buggy. Driving a fresh team of horses, he whipped them into a frenzy in the heart of the Allegheny Mountains as he set out for the Catskills of New York. They had left on Friday morning, and even though they had eventually allowed the horses to find their own pace, it was far from a leisurely trip.

In Livingston Manor, so close to their destination, they lost all restraint, stinging the flanks of the horses with a whip, driving them at a gallop along the shoulder of the highway, the spoke wheels spitting out gravel and sparks. Impatient, they left the road entirely and crossed a field, bypassing a half-mile of parked cars outside the Catalina Invitational.

Leaner, to all appearances, was wiping the sweat from his eyes after completing nine holes of play. Number Ten, 460 yards, par four, was now the object of his full attention as he tossed Jonah the towel.

But before the foursome could tee off, a solitary figure burst from the ranks of the gallery near the green and began to run toward them. It was John, the baron of the caddies' barracks, flailing his arms and shouting a warning to rival Paul Revere. The foursome could not get under way until he was off the fairway. He stumbled to the tee, out of breath and mumbling.

"Two men," John gasped, "they've come, they've come for..."

Catalina, who had been straddling the fender of his car at the edge of the tee, stood and slammed the open door.

"What is *this*? John, I've told you time after time

never to leave the barracks. Now you've gone and halted the whole tournament."

"But, but Max, Mister Catalina you don't understand. These two men, they have whips, they've come for—"

"Leo," Catalina barked. "Take John back to the barracks. It must be heat stroke."

Leaner didn't realize he was being warned...the quarter-mile sprint had drained the urgency from John's message. He walked the old man to the convertible, and John surrendered, allowing Fenner to drive him away. Before the engine started up, John turned to Leaner. "Look out, you scamp."

Scamp. Sherman stood by Leaner's side as they watched John's removal. "The poor old guy," Sherman said. "When it's time for me to go, I hope I go quick. Not like that."

"I think maybe he was trying to tell us something," Leaner said.

The foursome made their drives. Leaner, hitting last, placed his ball among the others but it was a fluke. He had tried incorporating the slice he'd been hitting on the last six holes, but instead of slicing to the target area he hit the ball dead straight there.

Meanwhile, Jonah's father and grandfather, whose names were Isaiah and Jeremiah, had ransacked the barracks while John tried to inform the golfing community of their arrival. They were religious *and* emotional. And tampering with the family structure by an outsider upset them personally as much as it contradicted their fundamental beliefs. The strength of their convictions allowed, even dictated, that they overturn furniture, rifle chests of drawers and rip mattresses from bunk beds...in the course of which they happened upon Jonah's old clothing. His father held the scratchy material gingerly, his mouth dropping open in anguish, as if the pair of pants were all that remained of his son's legs, the shirt a fragment of his torso. He folded the clothes reverently and they returned to the buggy to seek out the one responsible for Jonah's demise....

Father and grandfather were nowhere to be seen by the time Fenner walked John into the trashed-out building. Fenner took the barracks in with an incredulous look. "By gum, John, your housekeeping has sure seen better days. When was the last time you swept?"

Leaner was sizing up his second shot from the middle of the fairway when his foursome was again interrupted, this time not by one man who might get hit by a stray ball but by a pair of horses and a buggy, the wheels of which were plowing ruts into the golf course. Isaiah and Jeremiah had driven to the closest hole from the barracks, and as their luck would have it, they had to travel no farther than Number Ten.

Catalina was aghast. "What in hell *now*?" he said.

Leaner, curious, remained near his ball to watch, and saw one of the figures point at him. He returned the greeting with a wave. The horses galloped, their mouths frothy. Still, Leaner stood his ground. The buggy drew nearer and nearer, and it was only when the men were close enough for Leaner to see their expressions that he felt threatened enough to try to escape. After all, a horse-drawn wagon bearing down on him was not to be ignored. With open-field running he evaded them as best he could, but even with a good back he was no match for a team of horses.

The buggy pulled to a stop, and Jonah's father ran Leaner down the last ten yards, tackling him in a sand trap. He lifted Leaner by the front of his shirt and, twirling him about, rammed him against the back of the carriage. Leaner felt his back crack.

"What have you done with my son?" the man demanded in an accent, throwing Leaner against the vehicle again.

Before Leaner had time to respond he was roughed up again, bounced against the buggy he had no idea how many times.

Members of the gallery interceded at this point, pulling the two men apart. Harsh words were being exchanged as Jonah squeezed through the crowd and stood before his father and grandfather holding Leaner's golf bag, unrecognized by them before removing his Panama hat and sunglasses. When they at last made him out, it was a tearful reunion, it being forgotten for the moment that Jonah had spent his time in the belly of the whale dressed as an Amish Mick Jagger. The relatives threw back a flap of canvas on the buggy, and there, newly exposed to the sun like pale beansprouts, lay two of Jonah's charges—a pair of pinheads whose appearance made the gallery recoil. Simultaneously the pinheads broke into wide grins.

"Ya-ya!" they cried joyously. "Ya-ya!" Which was their way of pronouncing Jonah's name.

Cameras were clicking from the gallery. Now Catalina confronted the scene, walking slowly and deliberately along the ruts formed by the metal-rimmed wheels. He circled the carriage, inspecting the horses, one of which stamped a foot at Catalina's presence. Leaner was sitting on one of the buggy's running boards while Jonah was engaged in a spirited conversation with the two elders.

"What are they saying?" Catalina asked Leaner, unable to decipher the words.

"Could there be a chiropractor in the gallery?" Leaner said, looking at the ground.

"I can't make out what they're saying," Catalina repeated.

Leaner looked up. "It's German," he said. "I don't speak German, so don't ask me what they're talking about."

Catalina raised the bullhorn, aiming it like it was a pistol. "YOU TWO GENTLEMEN," he broadcast, "CONSIDER YOURSELF UNDER HOUSE ARREST."

Leaner stood and wrestled the bullhorn away from him. "For crying out loud, don't do that. Just don't do *anything.*"

"But these vandals have caused damage in the thousands," Catalina protested. "Look at poor old Number Ten."

"You can fix the fairway by just pressing down the edges of the ruts with your shoes, or at most a roller," Leaner said. "I've seen worse damage from divots. But there's no reason to be so damn loud. These people will probably be on their way as soon as they straighten out whatever it is they're talking about."

Jonah climbed down from the buggy, wringing his hands on the brim of his Panama hat. "Mister Leaner, I am forced to return home. Little Seth has not taken

food since my departure, and others among the pinheads are not well."

"Don't let them blackmail you into going back,
Jonah," Leaner told him. "Choose between the two. I
mean, your home life or this. Don't do anything you
don't want to."

"My life in Pennsylvania is sheltered, strict and
plain," Jonah said. "Since leaving home, I have blinded
my eyes with television, I have inhaled foreign drugs
through my nose, and last night I danced to modern
music and had sex with a woman."

"So you're staying?"

"I cannot lead a life free of responsibility," Jonah said,
climbing into the buggy. "I owe you money before I
leave."

"Keep it. You earned it."

Everyone watched them drive away, and Catalina
grabbed his bullhorn back when they were fifty yards
away. "PLEASE STAY ON THE CART PATH," he
blasted. Some of the gallery, thinking that the incident
was one of Catalina's renowned stunts, applauded the
performance.

Shorn of his caddy, Leaner was about to lift his clubs
for the resumption of play when a hand restrained his
forearm.

"Let me take those," Margot said. "I'll caddy for you
the rest of the way."

"That would be great. Thanks."

"How's your back?"

"I hadn't thought about it until just a minute ago,
but I think that guy fixed it when he beat the tar out
of me. Strange therapy, but my back doesn't hurt at all
any more."

19

AFTER THE DELAY, LEANER located his ball between the ruts left by the buggy. Had he not fled, the thing surely would have run him down. It took a few minutes for the foursome to reorganize itself, and the gallery had to be coaxed like some gigantic amoeba from the field of play. The confusion had blocked the golf course like a bad traffic jam, the groups playing behind Leaner's foursome unclear about what had happened but stalled in their progress. When Leaner, Sherman, Reasoner and Hollingsworth took their next shots, momentum was restored to the logjam.

Leaner had a better feel for the rest of Number Ten, but the sudden lifting of the handicap of his bad back also required some adjusting. On the front nine his back was at sixty percent, on the back nine he was closer to ninety. But he knew that backs didn't come in fractions. You either had one or you didn't.

The foursome regrouped on the next tee for the first time since the incident with Jonah's family. "Where were you guys when I needed help out there?" he said to his partners. "For all I knew, I was about to be murdered. I didn't see anybody lending a hand."

"I tried to get to you," Sherman said. "The crowd cut me off."

"Me too," Reasoner said. Leaner had seen him observing clouds during the ruckus.

"How about you, Buck?" Leaner asked Hollingsworth.

"As a celebrity, my life has been threatened more than once," Hollingsworth said. "I took the sensible precaution of maintaining a low profile."

"You ran," Leaner said.

Hollingsworth shrugged. "I had to protect the lead I was about to take," he said. "I *am* leading now, you know."

"Let's see what you do with it." Leaner smiled at him.

The fairway in front of them was wide open because the foursomes up there had continued to play during the delay. Catalina strolled up to them now.

"What is this? A golf tournament or a gabfest?"

Sherman had already teed up, and made his shot as soon as he heard Catalina open his mouth.

"And how is Leaner treating my little honey pie?" Margot was asked.

"Just fine, granddaddy," the sweet thing said.

Catalina stood right in front of Leaner as he was sizing up Number Eleven. "Have I mentioned before that this is my little honey pie?" he said, giving Margot a peck on the cheek, then strolling away with her, an arm snuggled around her waist.

"Come back here," Leaner said. "Y'all have my damn clubs."

She squirmed loose of him, and Catalina seemed content to stand on the edge of the tee, as if assaulting the foursome and making off with one of its caddies was no inconvenience whatsoever.

"Poor form," even Hollingsworth admitted.

Number Eleven was the relatively short par four, 369 yards long. Leaner hoped at least to par out the rest of this final round, with possible birdies on the par-three Twelve and Fifteen. The scenario might still bring him in the winner.

He made a fine drive. It felt good from the instant he started the downswing, and there was no pain in his back as he hit and followed through. The others had either driven to the short hair at the edge of the fairway or into the rough, so Leaner and Margot were alone in the middle of the fairway.

"Nine iron, please," Leaner said.

"You forgot to say 'May I.'"

"Gimme my goddam nine iron, goddammit. I'm trying to rebuild my momentum."

Margot removed the club from the bag, slowly extending it to him. "The animal in me is anxious to make love again," she said. "What does the animal in you feel like?"

Leaner made his shot, the ball landing and sticking on the green thirty feet from the pin. He returned the club. "This animal needs to make par, not love. Give me a break."

Leaner punctuated the statement with a sneeze. He was encouraged that nothing came of it this time.

Margot's tricky response was part laugh, part pout. "My man's animal better get his priorities straight."

Leaner ignored it, concentrating on canning his long putt. He didn't, but at least his par kept him within a stroke of Hollingsworth.

Twelve was the shorty par three overlooking a pond. Leaner's eight iron was right on the flag, but the ball pulled up short, and he had to tap in for another par.

Hollingsworth proceeded to throw his game into overdrive and string together birdies on Twelve, Thirteen and Fourteen. He was amazing to watch. Still, Leaner felt at this point that he was every bit as good as Hollingsworth, but he only managed a series of pars, thereby falling further and further behind. He was hanging in, but that wasn't good enough. He voiced a mild complaint to Margot, wondering how he could ever regain the lead with the way Hollingsworth was playing.

"You beat everybody there was for three days," she reminded him. "That's not anything to sneeze at. Sorry."

"This isn't a car race. They don't pay you for how many laps you were ahead."

Everybody had birdied Fourteen but Leaner. Fifteen was the shortest on the course. Leaner watched Sherman and Reasoner drive onto the green with nine irons. Hollingsworth, chatting with some of the gallery, seemed to bound up to the tee, knocking off a shot six feet from the pin. There was a burst of applause from the gallery. Hollingsworth was like a movie star. He gave a great performance. You had to give him that. Offscreen, though, you wanted to punch him out.

Leaner was now four strokes off the pace, with four holes remaining, including Fifteen. He knew Hollingsworth wasn't about to cave in and hand him the lead. He didn't want him to.

He landed on the green, fifteen feet from the hole, and two-putted for a par. Hollingsworth barely missed his birdie putt, but he did miss. Sherman and Reasoner, playing for pocket money by this time and under no pressure, both birdied.

Sixteen was the 569-yard par five, the longest hole on the course. It was bounded by three lakes, with sand traps like the surface of the moon—the bitch of the Catskills. If Leaner needed room to pick up a stroke or two, this was certainly the place to do it. He realized that it might be his last shot at the tournament title. Hollingsworth always had Kodak to fall back on, or his guaranteed cut of the gate. Golf was all Leaner had going for him. He gripped his driver, never loosening his grip while he waited out the other three.

Leaner then hit possibly the best tee shot of the entire tournament. He was so pleased with it that he lifted Margot off her feet and made a turn through the air with her, kissing her in plain view of the gallery and Catalina. He also called out to Hollingsworth, "And what would Ben Hogan have to say about that, Buck?"

"He'd say it was a very very good shot. I must admit that you've played as well as anyone I've beaten all year."

On the way to his second shot Leaner heard Margot sniffling as she carried his bag, turned and saw the tears running down her face.

"Don't cry—"

"I can't help it," she said, muffling her words through the sobs. "When you kissed me I realized that you were leaving forever, and I can't help it."

"I never strung you along," he said, "I never promised you anything."

"What?"

Leaner immediately realized he was sounding flip, but was too concentrated on his second shot to clear that up with her now.

"My two iron, please," he said. He hoped Margot's grief wouldn't carry her away, that he wouldn't have to wrestle her down for his clubs.

Since Leaner had outdriven the others, he was the last to take his second shot. He hit a long low ball that bounced for seventy-five yards after it landed. It was struck so well it dribbled into the trap adjacent to the green.

"At least you kept it out of the water," Margot said.

"I'm still in hot water," Leaner muttered to himself.

The gallery was getting excited again, sensing the eighteenth hole just around the bend. The standing ovation pumped up Leaner even more. It was as if the crowd was following only him, and it made him feel a little like Moses—Lord, what a presumptuous notion, he thought.

"Knock it out of there," Sherman told him as he entered the sand.

Leaner hit down on the ball, just hoping to get it out of the trap. There were slopes and plateaus to the green, and when the ball landed it rolled as if it was in a gravity house, curving left, then bee-lining straight for the hole. It hit the pin and bounced only six inches away. Margot promptly lifted the flag and Leaner tapped in for his first birdie of the day.

Hollingsworth parred, but still held a three-stroke lead with two holes to go.

Sherman told Leaner on Seventeen, "I'd almost given

up on you for a while, but you're back in this thing.
Kick ass, buddy."

At Seventeen, Hollingsworth's tee shot almost landed
on top of Leaner's. They played out the hole neck-and-
neck, each man making a par four. Hollingsworth's
three-stroke lead going into the final hole looked commanding, though Leaner tried to tell himself he had
seen larger gaps than that erased. He'd seen it, matter
of fact, earlier in the day.

Looking ahead to when it would be all over, Leaner
figured that everyone would go in a hundred different
directions at the grandstand, so at the eighteenth tee
he got in his goodbyes and thanks while he had the
chance. He was, it occurred to him, behaving like a
departing party guest with a bladder about to explode.

"Ray, a pleasure to play with you," he told Reasoner,
pumping his hand. "Sherman, thanks for your help,
especially today, and for showing me some of the ropes
up here. I hope the convention goes well for you in
Omaha." He found Catalina in the crowd now. "I
wanted to let you know that this has been some experience for me. I've learned a lot. It's a little nerve-
racking at times, but then, what isn't?"

"You're most welcome." Catalina beamed, thinking
he had made a convert.

Hollingsworth was watching Leaner strafing the area
with his well-mannered remarks, and it had a distracting effect on him. He addressed his ball, annoyed, and
proceeded to drive into the woods. Leaner paid no attention to the shot, nor to the gasps of the gallery. He
teed up, made an adequate 250-yard drive, moved off
the tee without comment.

Hollingsworth was in trouble. He was left without direct access to the fairway, his only shot being to loft the ball high over the trees. He would have to sacrifice some distance—actually had to shoot back toward the tee—but it would at least put him back on the fairway. The net of it was that his second shot moved him scarcely a hundred yards closer to home.

Meanwhile Leaner was on the green in two, fifteen feet from the flag. If he made the putt there was an outside chance he'd catch Hollingsworth. He waited. The other three made their way forward slowly, and Leaner wanted to sprint ahead of them and get the last hole behind him before his stomach knotted up. Instead he had to watch his partners edge, bit by bit, to the green. He walked to the side of the grandstand, waited, broke out in a sweat.

Hollingsworth had done no worse than par on any hole that day, but now lay four to Leaner's two. Hollingsworth, away, putted first, rimmed the hole. The gallery moaned, periscopes bobbed in waves. Hollingsworth tapped in for a double-bogey six, a final round three-under-par 68.

Leaner could tie him with a birdie three. His hands were shaking from waiting so long. Sweat ran into his eyes. He sank his shoe into the grass. His mouth was dry. He stepped back and took a practice stroke, then approached the ball again. It was a slightly uphill putt of fifteen feet. Leaner gave it a good rap, closed his eyes.

After the gallery's roar, the first thing Leaner could hear was Catalina over his bullhorn, his voice excited, high-pitched. "SUDDEN DEATH, LADIES AND GENTLEMEN. FOR THE FIRST TIME IN THE IN-

VITATIONAL'S HISTORY WE HAVE A SUDDEN-
DEATH PLAY-OFF!"

Leaner was swept up with the crowd so quickly he
scarcely realized what was happening. As unconven-
tional as Catalina had been in the preliminaries, how
would he handle a sudden-death situation? Roman can-
dles at ten paces? A one-to-one polo match while riding
zebras? Ingesting of poison to see who would be the
first to die?

The whole grandstand now emptied onto the eighteenth green. Leaner almost became separated from
Margot once, but amid the confusion he managed to
tally his four-day total. It read: 63-61-70-80. Ten under
par. Leaner walked with his hand lightly on the back
of Margot's neck as she led the way, toting his bag. He
anticipated the first sudden-death hole as if it was a
new game. He was dirty and exhausted, but it was
important to him to get out there on the first play-off
tee with at least the sense of a clean start. He took a
cloth to the heads of his irons, cleaning off the rem-
nants of mud, grass and sand, groped in his bag for a
new ball, was astonished he had none left. What a pro!
The course had been rough on them; the used balls
were stained and scarred.

"Do you think you could wash off my balls for me?"
he asked Margot, instantly regretting he'd said it.

"Right here in front of all these people?"

He merely glared at her, watched as she smiled pret-
tily and went off to the hand-cranked ball-rinser, pumping the contraption up and down. "How's my stroke?"

Leaner was spared further snappy Margot-talk by
Catalina's announcement over the bullhorn: "IN A

MOMENT...WE SHALL PROCEED...TO THE FIRST HOLE...SUDDEN-DEATH PLAY DICTATES...THAT THE FIRST MAN TO WIN A HOLE...SHALL BE DECLARED WINNER...OF THIS YEAR'S MAX... CATALINA...INVITATIONAL...GOLF TOURNAMENT."

"Get *on* with it," Leaner said, to himself. "Jesus."

"IN THE EVENT...OF A TIE...AFTER THE FIRST HOLE...PLAY WILL RESUME...ON THE SECOND HOLE...AND...IF TIED ON THE SECOND...PLAY PROCEEDS...TO THE THIRD...AND SO ON...I NOW ASK...THAT THE PLAYERS...APPROACH ME...FOR FURTHER INSTRUCTION."

Leaner and Hollingsworth walked up to Catalina, both towering over the little man, and as he threw his arms around their shoulders they had to bend over to accommodate him.

"Nice going, boys. This is historic. No question. Now, shake hands."

"What the hell," Leaner said, reaching out and pumping Hollingsworth's hand one time.

A low rumble could be heard from the gallery. It had begun the moment Catalina had ended his interminable broadcast, swelling in intensity to a hungry growl. Leaner, with the honor, moved toward the tee to hit but had to stop on account of the crowd noise. The cacophony then lowered to a murmur.

Leaner addressed his ball, stroked a lovely drive in the direction of the dogleg. The gallery applauded. Hollingsworth strolled to the tee and outdrove Leaner on the other side of the fairway. The gallery poured in on the heels of the golfers as they marched down the fairway.

"This is neat," Margot told Leaner. "God, look at all the people."

"I have a favor to ask you," Leaner told her.

"Ask and it shall be yours."

"That shirt you have on—"

"It's yours, I know. You'll get it back."

"I just want you to undo the top button for me."

Margot looked down at the V-neck. There was only one button, which she unfastened. "Like this?"

They had arrived at Leaner's ball and he reached into his bag for a safe two iron. "Yes, just like that."

"But it's nothing, I mean, it's just a pullover shirt."

"It's perfect."

The gallery was silent while Leaner planted his feet, then made a fine approach, leaving only a short pitch to the hole. On the other side of the fairway Hollingsworth was studying his own second shot, and in a moment Leaner could see the ball flying just beyond his.

They trekked on, Hollingsworth's fans beginning a low chorus of "Buck...Buck..." Leaner and Margot moved to his ball. Once again Leaner was away, and so had to shoot first.

"What do you want now?" Margot asked. "The nine or the eight?"

"The nine," Leaner said, taking it from her. "One more thing. Do you think you can do something with your hair? Maybe tie it back? Do you have a barrette you could pile it up with?"

"I don't think so. Is it that important?"

"It's important."

Margot reached down to one of the pockets of Leaner's bag, fished out a tee, wrapped her hair around a knot and planted the tee in the middle of it like a bobbypin.

Leaner watched without even a glance at the green ahead of him. "That's fantastic," he said.

He chipped to the green, the ball stopping just four feet short of the hole. Hollingsworth's attempt mirrored Leaner's. They were nearly equidistant from the flag, Leaner with an uphill putt, Hollingsworth with a downhill one.

"Thanks, Margot," Leaner said as they moved onto the green.

"What do you want me to do *now*?" she asked.

Leaner examined the break. It didn't look too bad. "I think I can handle this one on my own," he said.

He read a slight break to the left. Hollingsworth would be able to school on Leaner's shot for a better idea of his own putt, but Leaner didn't mind. He was happy to go first. If he sank it, the monkey would then be on Hollingsworth's back to match him.

He gave it a solid rap, and the putt dropped. Now Hollingsworth squatted down, closed one eye, lining the putter toward the hole. He stood up, crouched, stroked. His ball rolled, rolled, lipped the cup and was in. Halved in birdies.

"PROCEED...TO HOLE NUMBER TWO," Catalina intoned.

It would be the twentieth tee shot of the day. Margot, not wanting to interfere with Leaner's concentration, waited for his word as she hovered nearby.

"Can you maybe tuck your shirttail in a little?"

She did, smoothing out the wrinkled fabric with the palms of her hands. Leaner gave her a thumbs-up sign, then faced his ball and drove it two-seventy-five out onto the fairway. He joined her on the side while Hollingsworth got ready to shoot.

"What's with you and my clothes?" Margot wanted to know.

He shrugged. "I'm not sure.... it's just that somehow the whole picture is the deal. Like one of those Zen things. I appreciate you humoring me about it. It's not anything I should have to depend on, but it just *feels* right to me." A strange comment, he thought, for someone whose approach to the game, to life, had always been so controlled, so rational. What was going on?

Leaner and Hollingsworth might as well have been playing the same ball. Where one of them shot, the other followed. Leaner got into trouble on the second play-off hole, landing in a bunker. It looked bad for him until Hollingsworth plugged one right beside him. They were forty feet from the hole.

"Let's see," Leaner said. "I'll need my wedge... and is it possible to hike up the hem of that skirt of yours? An inch, tops."

Margot tugged on her waistband. Now her shirt was unbuttoned, her hair piled high, the shirttail pulled down and the dress edged up. No Zen here... those few extra millimeters of leg were what Leaner was after now.

"That's it," he told her. He pitched out of the trap, spraying sand across the edge of the green. The ball plopped down three feet from the cup for another almost certain birdie.

Now Hollingsworth stood in the bunker. He looked up at the flag, then back at his ball, then back to the flag once more. He positioned his feet in the sand, then chopped downward with an axlike stroke—a haywire improvisation, in Leaner's opinion. Somehow, though, the ball skyrocketed into a nearly vertical launch, hit a point at the apex of its flight and dived to the green. It bounced one time... and rolled into the hole.

Tension released in the gallery, and in the middle of it all Buck Hollingsworth was joyously spirited away.

Leaner stood there for a moment with his putter, ready to go for another birdie, a shot he would never make in the face of Hollingsworth's winning eagle. He felt rather foolish, though he knew he had no reason to. Margot didn't know what to say, except to invite him to ride back to the club in Catalina's convertible.

"That's okay," Leaner told her. "I think I need to walk this thing off."

"Will I see you later?"

"I guess."

"LADIES AND GENTLEMEN... WE THANK YOU FOR YOUR ATTENDANCE... SOUVENIR PROGRAMS ARE STILL AVAILABLE IN THE CLUBHOUSE... PLEASE DRIVE CAREFULLY... ON YOUR WAY HOME."

Leaner shouldered his golf bag, no longer surrounded by the crowd, only a member of it. He had walked about a hundred feet toward Catalina's club when a man in a Hawaiian shirt passed. Then, looking back over his shoulder at Leaner, the man shouted: "How does it feel to be a loser?

"How's it feel being a horse's ass?"

The man shot the finger at Leaner and ran off.

By the time he got to the clubhouse Leaner felt under control. After all, he had accomplished what he'd set out to do. He had played in a pro tournament. And had missed the championship by a fluke shot. Margot's thighs were lovely but not magic. He sat down at a table. In another part of the huge room he could see Leo Fenner pouring a bottle of champagne over Buck Hollingsworth's head. Leaner had someone bring him a beer.

Sherman appeared, pulling out a chair. He already had started on his own beer.

"Nine hundred and fifty dollars," he said, and Leaner's heart sunk, thinking for a moment that that was his winnings. "I checked the tote board. That's my take."

"Oh, well, I guess that's not too bad," he told Sherman, relieved. "I mean it's only for four days work."

Sherman raised the beer bottle to his lips and turned it upside down, draining the contents. He stood up and burped. "Well, so long, pal. You'll get him next time. You know, you're a real talent. I've enjoyed it. And I'll be watching for you in the funny papers."

Leaner signed a few autographs; two people even wanted to pose for photographs with him. Half an hour passed, and Catalina finally arrived, flanked by Fenner and a representative of a bank from New York City. The banker was on hand to draw up certified checks for the golfers' winnings. Hollingsworth was first to draw his pay and waved the check for the cameras. Then Leaner's name was called, and he stood in front of them feeling like he was being discharged from the army. He watched them set the figures on the check-writing machine, roll a bar across the face of it, and a piece of paper was presented to him. A cashier's check for $18,500.

"There you go," Catalina said. "I thank you, Thurmond, for a thrilling finish."

"This is a certified check that you can't stop payment on, isn't it?" Leaner asked quietly.

Catalina glared. "I want you at the press conference later."

Leaner folded the check into his pocket as he walked out of the building.

In his cabin he had turned on the television while he packed his suitcase. A newsman, substituting for the regular anchor, was wrapping up the evening news....

"Briefly, today in Roscoe, New York," Leaner heard him say, as he held a pair of socks in his hand and watched the set, "golfer Thurmond Leaner was almost run over by a horse-drawn buggy. A man climbed out of the buggy and demanded Leaner's caddy. Leaner answered, 'You can have him.' And he took him. From Washington, good-night."

Leaner unplugged the TV set and went out the door with his luggage and clubs, throwing his things in the back seat as he slid behind the wheel. Margot caught him just as he started the engine. She banged on the glass and Leaner cranked down his window.

"Please, *please* take me with you."

Leaner took a good look at her. She was attractive as could be, though he still wondered if she weren't younger than she admitted to. For a moment he imagined driving off with her, only to be picked up and arrested for a violation of the Mann Act. He felt awful about it, and though he doubted she would believe it, in a way it was harder on him than on her. But even Zen had its limits, as he'd just found out. He stepped on the gas and drove on out of there.

20

"THIS IS THURMOND LEANER,
in 804. I'd like to make a long distance call to area code
713. The number is 488-0499."

"Do you want that billed to your room or is it collect?"

"Go ahead and bill me for it."

He listened to the clicks of the circuits as the con-
nections to Texas were thrown open. Leaner loved the
idea that his voice would be racing along the wires like
an express train. Lauren answered his call.

"Hi," Leaner said. "Has the monkey found its way
home?"

"One's still missing," she said. "The other's in New
York. Who is this?"

"He's not in New York anymore," Leaner said. "He
couldn't stand the Catskills a moment longer and drove
to the Holiday Inn in Danbury, Connecticut."

"How did he do in the tournament?" Lauren asked.

"He came in second, winning a purse of eighteen
thousand five hundred dollars. He's going to Boston in

the morning, and he'll wire the money to Houston from there."

"That's *great*, Thurmond. I had my doubts, but this is just how you dreamed it would be. You played well, and you won a lot of money. It makes me happy."

"It was hard work," Leaner said. "I've got that agent's name from Amelia, too. I'll be looking him up in Boston tomorrow. Would you like to meet me in Boston?"

"I'd better not. A couple of kids in the neighborhood spotted Bingo yesterday, so he's still in the area. He might come back."

"Where was he?"

"He was eating from a bird feeder, then ran down a telephone cable. The kids chased him with their bikes, but he cut them off at that drainage ditch a few streets over."

"I'll buy you another monkey if that's what you want. I'll buy you a barrel of monkeys."

"I just want Bingo. Thurmond, I want you too. It's just that that little furry animal has a way of stealing into your heart, and I'm worried about him." Her voice trailed off. "He's so helpless out there," and she began to cry.

"I'm sorry, take it easy."

"Call me from Boston and let me know what's going on, okay?"

"I will, and when I get home we'll go to that restaurant you like in Galveston. We'll check in to the Flagship for a few days if you want."

"Don't get preoccupied with what I want," she said. "Just come home as soon as you take care of your business and we'll be partners again, all right?"

Leaner never felt more like a swine than when he hung up the phone. He knew that Lauren would likely refuse his invitation to Boston if the monkey was still missing. And chances were it would be. But he asked her anyway. After his transgression with Margot Catalina, a vague promise of a meal and a hotel overlooking the Gulf of Mexico seemed contemptible to him.

He changed into a swimsuit and did a few laps in the motel pool. When he had nearly exhausted himself, he stood in the shallow end, not being so hard on himself about Lauren. "I'm a fairly decent guy, all in all," he said, wiping his hair and water from his eyes.

In the morning he slept late, showered, checked out and was on the road to Boston. He was glad he'd spent the night in Connecticut, certain that if he'd stayed any longer in Catalina's cabins, or even in the State of New York, the Catskills would have woven more of their madness onto him. He figured he'd gotten out just in time.

It seemed like the seasons had changed since he'd driven a car, and Leaner couldn't get over the scaled-down distances he was encountering as he traveled ever farther east. New York, Connecticut and Massachusetts—or, more colloquially, the Empire State, the Land of Steady Habits and the Bay State—seemed no larger than state parks to him.

He left the highway in Hartford, Land of Steady Habits State Park, had a light lunch and drove down Farmington Avenue, passing slowly in front of the magnificent homes of Mark Twain and Harriet Beecher Stowe, next-door neighbors at one time. As a semiskilled framer and carpenter himself, he admired and appreciated the handiwork that must have gone into the homes.

He turned sharply north, and when he encountered the Massachusetts Turnpike he could practically smell Boston at the end of it. He drove on, and after paying his toll in the mass of towns he assumed to be Boston, he entered the city. He came upon rotaries, circling islands of traffic he had no experience with, that sent him spiraling in directions he hadn't wanted to go. When he thought he'd found his bearings again, another rotary would appear, six streets converging like the spokes of a wheel, and off he was sent again, swirling around obstacles like a leaf in a stream, blending with travelers of adjoining tributaries, seemingly aimless but moving in one general direction.

Figuring he was in the heart of the city, he found a parking space and maneuvered into it. In fact, he was in Harvard Square in Cambridge, and at twenty-eight felt middle-aged. Pedestrians, other drivers, joggers, bicyclists, everyone Leaner could see looked no older than twenty. It was as if he had inadvertently driven into a restricted youth zone—which, of course, in a way he had, considering the cluster of colleges nearby: Harvard, M.I.T., Radcliffe.

He locked the car and walked across the Square in search of a pay phone. In the space of a block he passed three ice-cream vendors and ten times that number of their customers. To live in Boston, Leaner was beginning to think, one must be young and, to stay young, jog with an ice-cream cone.

He ducked into a cheesecake shop when he saw its phone from outside, lifted the receiver and dug through his wallet for Amelia's agent's number. The aroma of the shop was overpowering, and before Leaner put his coins in the phone he ordered a slice of cheesecake, drowned it in strawberry topping and sat in a booth by the window. After the first bite he wanted to rush to the doorway of the shop and curb one of the ice-creamers as they jogged past to let them know they were missing a bet on the cheesecake. It was ambrosia.

Leaner polished it off quickly and returned his attention to the telephone. Holding the number in the palm of his hand, he listened to the agent's phone ring. If he had any qualms about the validity of golfers being sole recipients of funny names, they were dispelled when the agent's receptionist answered.

"Bluestocking, Ludlow, Epps and Moon," she sang.

"Yes, is Mister Epps in?" Leaner asked, his voice coming out thickly, thanks to a delicious film of cheesecake paste lining his mouth.

"Who is calling, please?"

"Thurmond Leaner."

"One moment."

While he was on hold, he imagined the receptionist and the agent trying to decipher who he was, debating whether to leave him on hold until he gave up or to answer immediately to chew him out for calling anonymously. He was taken off hold.

"Thurmond, it's wonderful to hear from you," Epps said.

"You know who I am?"

"Certainly. Amelia called, when was it? Oh, last Thursday or Friday. She was going out to Martha's Vineyard to visit with Carly. Where are you now, Thurmond?"

Leaner looked out the window. "On the corner of Church and Palmer."

"You're in town, then. Wonderful. Are you dropping by the office?"

"I guess so," Leaner said. "You want to tell me how to get there?"

"Surely. You're in Harvard Square now. Are you familiar with Boston?"

"Not at all."

"Just get on the subway at Harvard Square, the Red Line. The routes are color-coded, so you can't miss it. Take the Red to the Park stop and get out. Don't transfer."

"The Red Line to Park," Leaner echoed.

"That's right. When you come out on the street you'll be right at our office. We're on the corner of Park and Tremont. You have the Tremont Street address?"

"Yes."

"Wonderful. We'll see you shortly. Phone if you get lost."

"I will."

Leaner glanced at his parked car as he entered the subway complex and hoped it would still be there when he returned. He had never ridden on a subway and was a little worried that he might get it all wrong. He could somehow miss his stop, or be waylaid by subterranean gangs whose members took turns lifting him by the throat with one hand, slamming him into support pillars just to see his out-of-town eyes rattle.

The train pulled in to the station and he got aboard. There was, though, a scramble for the seats, and Leaner wasn't fast enough. He was, in fact, astonished that a crowd could move so quickly. He had to ride standing up, and proceeded to study the map on the wall, seeing how far it was to his stop. The air was a mixture of diesel and sweat, but he still enjoyed the ride as a new experience. When the train broke clear of its tunnel, bursting into the daylight to cross the Charles River, Leaner ducked to peer out a window. He was not, though, registering on particulars.

Once on foot again, he could have retraced Paul Revere's ride, stepped on the space where Crispus Attucks had dropped dead in his tracks, or stood staring at the State House...and he would not have known what he was looking at. He had but one sightseeing goal at the moment: to find Epps.

21

"THURMOND, YOU MAY HAVE
noticed during our telephone conversation that I use
the word 'wonderful' quite a bit. 'Fabulous' is another
favorite around this office." Epps began to count on his
fingers now. "We're involved with theater people, rock
stars, movie stars, authors and the lecture circuit, where
you'll run the gamut from Henry Kissinger to G. Gor-
don Liddy. We provide for commercial advertisements.
TV spots, radio spots, spreads in magazines and newspapers. If a person or product is presented to the public,
we're right there in the wings. I've seen careers sky-
rocket, and there's nothing in this world like being a
part of it. I haven't considered another line of work
since my first bite in this business. It's made a life for
me that's, well, wonderful. Fabulous."

His trip to the office being uneventful, he somehow
figured that Epps would be a down-to-earth, rational
and unassuming character, not the sparkler he found
burning brightly before him now. He had deliberately
bailed out of the Catskills and their frenzy, and had

been looking ahead to some level-headed Bay State normality.

"Is Amelia still in Martha's Vineyard?" he asked.

"Oh, no," Epps was quick to answer. "It was a day, day-and-a-half visit with Carly, then she was off for rehearsals for a fall tour. What a wonderful sister you have, Thurmond."

Leaner smiled uneasily. "I'm glad I could come by and meet you," he said, "but I have a long drive ahead of me and I'd best be moving on."

"Whatever are you saying? I have work for you immediately, if you're interested. Amelia filled me in on your background, and I've just the thing. Let's go to Faneuil Hall, hoist a few tankards of ale and kick it around."

"All right," he said, getting caught up in Epps' go-get-'em spirit.

As they passed the receptionist, Epps told her, "Missy, if an emergency comes up we'll be hoisting a few at Faneuil Hall. Try to keep the ship on a steady course."

Missy, simultaneously wired up to take dictation from a cassette and answer the phone through a headset, looked like she could handle any number of ships. She nodded, stopped typing and, adjusting her earpiece, crooned to a light blinking on the panel before her, "Bluestocking, Ludlow, Epps and Moon." Leaner was fascinated.

They walked into the sun, and although Leaner was taller and ten years the younger of the two, he found himself walking faster than normal to keep pace with Epps. Epps led him into the subway, and they got on board a train just as it was closing its doors. "This is the Green Line," he told Leaner in a voice loud enough to draw stares. And when they transferred routes he called out, "We're on the Blue Line now. The routes are color-coded."

"I know," Leaner called back.

On street level again, Epps became a mini-tour guide. But rather than show Leaner various pieces of history, he would merely point in their general direction. "We're in the old part of the city," Epps said. "Over there"— he aimed a finger—"is the Old North Church. You know, one if by land, two if by sea. And there's where the Boston Tea Party happened. The State House is close to the office but the Old State House and City Hall are right around the corner. Right ahead is Faneuil Hall."

Leaner wasn't too impressed. He understood that being familiar with the background of a building, knowing who ate or died there in times past, could add all the charm necessary to transform a shack into a palace. Excellent food would also do the trick, but Leaner wasn't planning on dinner there. Also, he had never heard of the place, which he wasn't about to tell Epps. Later he would learn that Faneuil Hall was once Benjamin Franklin's hangout, or so it was said, and that *did* excite him.

When they found a table, Leaner asked Epps what kind of work he was planning for him.

"You might find it hard to believe," Epps said, "but I think you'd be wonderful in TV commercials. You might be fabulous. All you athletes, you golfers in particular, are such blond, tan and healthy Americans that when you stand behind a product the American housewife in her daydreams just can't help running out and buying as much of that product as she can lift. Men will want it too, because they're jealous of you and want to have what you have. And that accent of yours. Thurmond, you'll make the ladies swoon."

"I didn't think I had much of an accent," Leaner said, "and I'm not blond."

"Listen to him." Epps laughed, beating the table with his fist. "Ah dinnunt know ah hid a ack-sint. *Fabulous.*"

"Come off it," Leaner said. "You make it sound like I'm about to break into a chorus of 'Ol' Man River.'" He drained half of his beer.

"Listen to me, Thurmond, what we've developed are several categories that all commercials can fit into, accent or no accent. Right now a real popular item is the testimonial on hidden camera. You don't have expensive props to arrange and you generally have no more than two or three actors to pay. See, you bring in a guy, supposedly off the street but in fact a member of the Screen Actors Guild. He says his head hurts, he describes the pain. He's given, say, an aspirin and he later says that aspirin was the only thing that has ever made his boomer of a headache go away. Here's Mister Average, and he has his finger on the pulse of the nation, so to speak, and he's celebrating your product. Another approach is the informed acquaintance. You must have seen these. A woman in a store can't make up her mind over what kind of toilet paper to buy. There are *so* many to choose from. Does she want perfumey toilet paper? Rose-colored? Plaid? Okay, she buys an inferior brand, but before making it to the checkout counter she runs into a friend who has the lowdown on the best toilet paper on the planet Earth. This friend makes her return the bad toilet paper to the shelf and gives her a roll of the good stuff. Very effective, believe me. Advertising agencies usually get in touch with us, and we line up the people for the commercial."

"What other kinds are there?" Leaner asked. "I'd feel like a fool in one of those."

"I agree," said Epps, "although you might be a hidden camera man. But I guess that would be stretching things. How about the irrelevant demonstration. Say you want a great paper towel. How do you find the best? Simple. You wet down the one you're selling, and you do the same to the competitor. You can even name the competitor if you want. After you get them soaked, you see how many eggs you can hold in them before they fall apart. Well, the competitor shreds, and you have broken eggs all over the floor, and to clean up the mess you use the paper towel you're pushing. A better paper towel will hold more eggs. But that isn't what you buy a paper towel for, is it? It's an irrelevant demonstration. Timex has always advertised this way, doing this and that to wristwatches, and they're very successful with it."

Leaner couldn't picture himself involved in such shenanigans. "What else?" he said, gulping the beer.

"Oh, waitress," Epps called, "two more tankards of ale over here. Now, Thurmond, keep in mind that these are basic categories. You can combine them and get hybrids, like an irrelevant hidden camera. My favorite form is very basic. It just presents the product and shows what it does, like a good tire commercial. It'll show you how the tire is constructed, and what it will do in all kinds of weather and road conditions. But whether it's tires or ballpoint pens, it's good to have an eye-catcher to grab the viewer's attention. Driving a car through a paper banner is a good eye-catcher. You can use that with anything. A hang glider is a good eye-catcher too. Ten years ago you'd use a surfboard, but today it's hang gliders. You generally rely on an eye-catcher if you don't have much to say about the product, like chewing gum. Of course, you could just throw one in for emphasis. Understand, I'm only scratching the surface of all of this.

"Now we come to where you fit in. It's a variation on the eye-catcher—"

"Hold it, I'm not jumping off any cliff holding on to an oversize kite."

"No, no, no." Epps laughed. "I'm talking about the celebrity endorsement."

"But I'm not a celebrity. I came in second."

"Celebrities are made, just like gingerbread men. And once your golf career takes off, and I have every reason to believe that it will, your celebrity status will rise proportionately. Look, when Buck Hollingsworth says he uses Kodak film, it makes people want to go out and buy Kodak. This appeal goes back ages and no one has ever come up with anything that's more success-ful."

"It's funny you should mention Buck Hollings-worth," Leaner said. "He just edged me out in the Catalina Invitational."

"Don't you mean the Catalina Memorial?"

"No, the Invitational."

"Max Catalina? The last I heard of him he was ne-gotiating with California to buy Catalina Island. At least he made headlines. Great publicity gimmick. At any rate, if Buck Hollingsworth can fatten his income with an auxiliary career, so can you. He flies his own jet, you know. I'm going to have Missy run down all of your press coverage from the Catalina and we can build on that. Maybe start you out with regional coverage, then work our way national—"

"But I thought you said you already had some work for me."

"I do, and from what your sister says, it's your field of expertise."

"Well, what is it?"

"It's my house on Cape Cod. I need a little remodeling, and I'd really like you to look at it. You could work on it and stay in it while we run down the best scenario for launching your auxiliary career."

Leaner had a sinking feeling. All the talk and energy Epps had used had apparently been only to lure him into some work on his house. "I don't know. I just won over eighteen thousand dollars yesterday. The idea was to pursue a golf career and get away from the hammers and nails."

"What harm would there be in your looking at the house? I'd certainly value your suggestions. I could always get someone else to do the work but I'd like to hear what you have to say, I really would."

Leaner didn't want to insult the guy. He was, after all, his sister's agent. He finished his beer. "Tell me how to get to Cape Cod."

Leaner wired the golf money to his bank in Houston; then, in separate cars, he and Epps headed for Epps's house outside of Truro on Cape Cod. It was tricky getting out of Boston, but once they were on the right highway there was no way he could miss Cape Cod. For a minute, when Epps's car had gotten out of sight, he considered turning around and heading south, just letting Epps go on to his own house and wonder what became of him, but then decided it would be a kind of test to go through with the project. To work with his hands when he hadn't the financial need to work at all for a year was a curious blend of the Protestant work ethic and the inability to look a gift horse in the mouth. If nothing else, construction work—remodeling rich folks' homes, particularly—paid just about whatever you asked.

The house turned out to be fairly isolated, and its circular driveway defined nearly an acre of land. Leaner parked his car behind Epps's. The house looked fine to him. Most houses did. But it somehow fell short of Epps's notion of what he wanted.

Epps bounded out of the front door and welcomed Leaner inside. "I'll show you the area that needs help," he said, and led Leaner through the house and out a screen door in the back to a beautiful view of the bay. "It's right here," Epps said.

Leaner was marveling at the water. "How's the crabbing here?"

"I don't bother the crabs, and they don't bother me. Honestly now, what do you think of this back area?"

Since Leaner had already decided to take the job, he figured he would play with Epps a bit. Tit for tat. "It's all you really need," he said. "You have the back door, the screen door and the steps to the ground. There's nothing really *wrong* with it." He paused, then added, "But if it was *my* house I'd tear down the steps, run a deck coming out from the door and extending to that other room. That section of the house—what is it, a bedroom?"

"Yes."

"I'd put a trellis above the deck tying in to the deck's support posts. That would shade the area. You could tack up bamboo curtains that would cut the glare of the sun setting on the water. You'd cool off this whole side of the house and save on electricity. Put handrails in at waist level, add more steps and you'd have a nice living area out here."

"*Fabulous.* You don't know how this sets my mind at ease. I've had a couple of parties out here since I bought the house, and this whole back was just dead. Guests seemed almost scared of it, and the rest of the house was crowded on account of it."

"You might consider a sliding glass door, too," Leaner said. "I couldn't do that by myself, but I'll draw the plans if you want."

"Oh, don't fret about the sliding glass door," Epps said. "I guess I do need the deck and trellis, though. Can you, uh, estimate what it would run me?"

"No," Leaner said. "I'm familiar with wood prices in Houston but even they change from week to week. I could tell you what I'd charge if you supplied all the material."

"How much?"

Leaner paused again. He figured the job would take a week. "Eighteen hundred," he said off the top of his head.

Epps was quiet and Leaner thought he'd lost him.

"Well, you sold me. Before, I was really just thinking about it, but now I can't live without it. I'll leave you my credit cards to buy the material."

"Do you have any tools?"

"In the garage. There's a wheelbarrow out there and some other stuff."

"I'll need a posthole digger and a shovel," Leaner said. "I've probably got everything else I need in the trunk of the car. If I gave you a list, could you get the materials delivered out here tomorrow? No use in renting a truck."

"No problem," Epps said. "Do you need an advance?"

"Not if I'm staying here. But I do have a standard work contract I always carry with me out of habit. It will get the terms in writing. I'll be starting as soon as I have something to work with. I figure to be out of here in under ten days."

"Wonderful," Epps said. "Working in that time frame, Missy will get her research done, and Bluestocking, Ludlow, Epps and Moon will begin the countdown on the launching of Thurmond Leaner's auxiliary career."

"Sounds okay," Leaner said, not so sure.

"Indeed it does. I'm going back to the city tonight. I'll make sure the material is here by noon tomorrow so you can get started. Don't worry about the telephone. I write the whole thing off. Call Ecuador every day if you want. The freezer's full. Help yourself to the liquor. I'll touch base with you in the evenings."

Epps gave Leaner a spare housekey, then went back to Boston with the work contract and supply list.

Leaner walked inside, took a steak from the freezer, fixed a drink and watched the sun set on Cap Cod Bay. He wasn't sure how he felt at the moment, but there was something to the analogy of a gingerbread roasting in the oven that seemed to fit.

22

LEANER HAD USED THE
interstate highway system to make his trip north. From
Houston to Boston the only cities of any size he had
encountered had been Little Rock, Memphis and Nash-
ville, and he had driven through those without stopping. The rest of the country, if he was to judge it only
by the view from his car, was a panorama of farmland,
pastures, rivers, forests, hills and now, nearly as far as
he could travel eastward, bays and ocean.

When he opened the door to the hardware store the
following morning, he was greeted by the same hardware scent he knew at home. Even as a child he had
liked the smell. It was galvanized metal you could
almost taste, new tires, paint, tools, and perhaps
standard-smelling hardware clerks. It was so constant
a thing that if ever he should walk into a hardware
store that lacked the smell, he would figure that the
world had gone seriously awry.

He bought bolts and nails, inhaling deeply at the
counter. At home, to work outside in August, he would

be broiling by now. On Cape Cod, in the morning at least, he wore a long-sleeved shirt.

"I'm remodeling the Epps house," Leaner told the clerk.

The clerk bagged the items and shook them once. "A big job?"

Leaner shrugged, thanked the man and said he would be back. As he returned to the house a lumber truck was just leaving the driveway. It had dumped a bundle of wood, bags of cement, a posthole digger and a roll of plastic. He spent the next half-hour moving everything to the work area in back, using Epps's wheelbarrow to carry the cement. He had taken off his shirt by the time he was through. He then took out of his car trunk his extension cord, a drill, two electric saws and all the hand tools he had with him. He fastened his belt with its hammer and tape, its surplus nails and wood chisel, and set out to work.

Epps hadn't cared about seeing Leaner's plans, so Leaner hadn't bothered to draw any. He knew what he was doing and visualized the whole project laid out in steps, just as he did a golf round. He staked out the ground, squaring his corners with a reliable 3-4-5 right-triangle made of string. He could build a whole house without plans if he had to....

By the end of the day he had bolted two-by-sixes at floor and ceiling level against two walls of the house, into its studs. This would allow the house itself to support half of the new structure. He had dug the holes and set the posts in concrete, also aligning them with string. It was hot and dirty work and, after rinsing the wheelbarrow of excess cement, he held his head under the hose for a full minute. He then covered the wood with the plastic; he would let the four-by-fours set in the cement overnight before nailing onto them.

He took a shower and, marveling at the size of the bath tub, lay down and plugged the drain. There was room to stretch out completely, something Leaner had been unable to do in a tub since he became full grown. It felt wonderful to bathe without being cramped. "A fabulous tub," he said.

Epps phoned in the evening and said that Missy was still in the process of running down approaches to Leaner's publicity.

"You didn't tell me you were on the Nightly News," Epps said.

"I didn't know I was," Leaner lied, relieved that he hadn't imagined it.

"That's *excellent* PR," Epps went on. "The thing to do now is to volley with something else while you're still fresh in the public's mind, even if only subliminally. But we didn't have anything come in today that I thought would be right for you. There was something for a denture adhesive, and a public service announcement about the early warning signs of colitis. I want to get you something that's robust. You know what I mean?"

"I guess so," Leaner said.

"How's the work going? Did the material arrive?"

"It's fine," Leaner said. "The support structure will be finished tomorrow."

"That's *wonderful*," Epps said. "Be sure to call if you run into any snags."

Leaner prepared another steak for dinner and called Lauren afterward, paying, as directed, no heed to telephone expenses. They were at it for an hour. Leaner told her all he knew about Epps, about the commercial work that had been dangled before him, and about the work he was doing on Epps's house, which could come to thirty dollars an hour. There were fairly long gaps during which neither spoke. They tried to think of things to say but there wasn't that much news. The golf tournament was over, and the monkey was still missing.

In the morning Leaner nailed runners along the posts, then bolted them into place. At one point he wished his helper Garcia was there. There was a twenty-foot span to link and it was difficult for one man to do. So Leaner improvised. After building the perimeter of the deck, he covered the ground with a sheet of plastic to prevent the growth of weeds underneath the floor. He checkered the area with supports and decided to lay the floor. He spaced the boards at a quarter-inch, and since some of them were slightly warped he had to wrestle them into place with a crowbar. It developed into an afternoon of isometrics, and he was ready to drop by the time he finished. He languished again in the huge bathtub.

Epps did not call that evening. The following morning, Thursday, Leaner drove to the ocean and took a long walk along the beach, noting that here the sand was like gravel compared with the Texas coast. The water was violent. He could tell it was deep close to shore, and the waves looked like they could pull him right out to sea.

Leaner started to debate with himself. He had proved he could handle the golf stress, but was agreeing to remodel the Epps house a stall? It was summer, tournaments were scheduled every week. Playing as well as he did, he could make real money. But he'd looked no farther than the Catskills. Nothing had been easy there, he reminded himself, but was it so wrong not to challenge himself every time?

He drove back to the house and nailed two-by-twos across the trellis supports. With shade to work under, he built the steps, leaving only the handrails to do on Friday. Again, Epps did not call.

He slept late in the morning, and as he stepped outside he saw it was overcast and felt the unseasonable chill. He built the rails at his leisure, wearing a sweatshirt he had found in a closet. When he was through, he telephoned Epps's office.

"Your house is done," he said. "The deck and rails are smooth and the beams and trellis are all rough cedar."

"*Fabulous*," Epps said. "Listen, I have some news for you. Missy couldn't come up with much. It's been a real dog-and-pony show around the office all week. I wanted you to know that even though I didn't call I was thinking about you. We ran an analysis of your situation. We *made* the time for that. I'm sorry...."

"Exactly what are you saying?" Leaner said. He wanted Epps to put it into words.

"I guess it means I was wrong. The deal with the commercials fell through."

"I see."

"Say, while I've got you on the horn, I wanted to ask you...will the trellis support the weight of a few houseplants? I think they'd look great out there."

"It's well constructed," Leaner said. "Sturdy enough

to turn it into a gallows if you like. You can hang yourself from it and have room to spare for Bluestocking, Ludlow *and* Moon."

"I don't blame you for being upset," Epps said, "but you don't know this business like I do. Look, I'll drive out tonight with your check. All right?"

"You've got no class, Epps," Leaner said, and hung up. He wondered how Amelia could stand the creep.

He went outside, walking across the deck, climbed down the steps and began to pile the wood scraps into a heap. For a moment he thought of torching the trash and, if the flames got a little out of hand, making a halfhearted attempt to save Epps's house, then watching the whole pile get reduced to cinders.

The air was moist and cool, and he had yet to raise a sweat. When he finished he sat on the ground, looking at the addition to the house. At least he could take pride in it.

He felt something hit his hair, brushed at it with his hand. It was an enormous bird dropping, and he looked skyward to see a great blue heron winding toward the bay. He shivered and walked to the bathroom, his expression one of disgust—with Epps, with the bird, with, all of a sudden, himself. He looked like someone who had inadvertently taken a mouthful of sour milk and had no place to spit.

He lit the bathroom heater and washed his hands, then shampooed in the sink, too chilled to consider a bath. But he changed his mind. He used a blow-dryer he found in the cabinet while the tub filled with water. When he had dried his hair he stepped into the tub and lay down to relax. The water absorbed his chill.

"No class," he said. "Epps may have less than anyone

I've met since leaving home. Leo Fenner and Cousin Vernon have no class. Catalina maybe does, somewhere. I know Kid Doolin does. Margot Catalina, yes. Buck Hollingsworth, definitely not. Amelia, absolutely, but she has a lousy agent."

He lay back in the water a very long time, classifying people. He thought of his parents. "Why were they so old when I was born? I know I wasn't planned, but did they have to be so *old*, like grandparents? They were gone before I got to know them. Mother, I miss you, badly."

As he spoke Leaner became aware of a sensation in his mouth. It was like two hours after a visit to the dentist when one side of the face and mouth tingled. He felt his heart beating too fast and licked his lips. When he raised his right hand to feel his forehead, his arm felt prickly too. He lifted a leg out of the water. It felt cold, clammy and numb. Paralysis was tiptoeing across the right half of his body. He was scared. Was he having a stroke?

He turned his head quickly. The blow-dryer. The heater. There was no longer a flame, but still a hiss of gas. His heart now beat loud, boom-boom, in his ears; yellow splotches obscured his vision. He tried to lift himself from the water but found he hadn't the strength and slipped, his toes pulling the plug from the drain as he fell.

As the water around Leaner's body receded slowly, he felt himself going down the drain with it.

23

IT WAS A DREAM
to him, bridging a fitful sleep. He heard voices, familiar
ones. But they were out of context. They spoke with
each other when in fact they had never met. Then there
was silence and sleep, and howls, and sensations of
movement. He knew something had happened to him,
and if it was death, then death wasn't so bad. You just
couldn't open your eyes. The rest of it was voices.
Amelia's was the clearest. After all, she was a singer.
Lauren was in there somewhere, and even Margot.

He heard his mother, too, but that was part of the
dream. She had said, "Stand up, son. You left the gas
on in the heater. Stand up and fix it and I'll dry your
back."

Then he felt himself moving again, and he heard the
howls, which were the sirens of ambulances.

At last he knew he was awake. He could feel himself
lying in a bed. He could open his eyes when he wanted,
but first he listened. Muffled by distance, he heard...
"He's a spider monkey and he came from Costa Rica.

He was missing for over a week but I went out the other morning and he jumped out of a tree right into my hair. He lost weight while he was away but I still hope to make some money with him."

"You mean like an organ grinder?"

Leaner strained. He was sure that the second voice was Margot's, but the pair of them...Lauren, Margot ...together seemed impossible to him. He heard them walk down a hall, and he opened an eye. Was it dawn? Dusk? He didn't know, but the light was dim as it struggled through the window.

He threw back the sheets. Tubes were in his left arm, and his right was in a cast. A figure slept in a chair nearby. Leaner reached from the bed and pulled back its blanket.

"Amelia?" he said.

For a change, it was his turn to startle her. She jumped, then threw her arms around his neck and began to cry quietly.

"Is that who I think it is in the hall?" he asked her.

"Yes," she said, "and it seems they've become the best of friends."

"The heater went out," he told her, not adding that he found out about it in a dream. "I got gassed but it wasn't anything like a suicide try."

"I know," Amelia told him, smiling over-brightly. "Epps found you in the bath and called an ambulance. That's how you broke your arm. Epps dropped you. Thurmond, you have over a *thousand* telegrams and cards. People love you. Epps said you have your pick of a dozen endorsements. The accident has been in the papers for three days now."

"What day is it?"

"Tuesday. They thought it was a coma. Let me buzz for the nurse. She said to, when you regained consciousness."

"I've been dreaming...my head hurts and I might not make sense...I had a time in Florida and then in the Catskills, swore to myself I'd never go back to either place. And then Epps fell through for me on Cape Cod and I felt the same thing. I mean, imagine never wanting to see the Atlantic twice, or towns like Barnstable, Hyannis and Truro again. Amelia, I know it's irrational to blame a place for a state of mind. It's just a convenient damn thing to do.... But where do you draw the line? To one city, a neighborhood, a house? God...I don't want to be a recluse with a bunch of Mormons to pre-taste my food. But can it be all right to put the blame somewhere else when I know I'm responsible right down to the wire for whatever I do? Or am I like an alcoholic taking a geographic cure?"

Amelia pulled the covers around his chest and tucked in the sheet. "Of course it's all right," his sister said, wiping her face dry. "Of course it is."

"Then what the hell's bothering me so much?" He raised his voice. "Why do I feel so badly about doing so well in my first tournament, treating most people, if I may show a little conceit, at least as well and sometimes better than they treat me? There's something wrong, Amelia, and if I could put my finger on it, I would. If somebody would be kind enough to point it out to me, I'd be all ears. I said a while ago that this wasn't a suicide attempt. But deep down, I don't know ...maybe it was?"

Leaner lay his head back on the pillow and closed his eyes.

24

THE TV CAMERA WAS
anchored onto the platform high in the air. Hundreds
of cables snaked across the grass behind the bleachers
near the eighteenth green. The cables led to a parked
mobile truck that served as the broadcast command
post. People with clipboards were barking out orders,
but the flurry of activity gave the impression that no
single person was in charge. Within the RV, one man
wearing a headset pressed his back against his chair.
The wall in front of him was a bank of TV monitors.
Periodically he threw switches, changing positions
when he spoke into the mike attached to his headset.
He had been sitting for three days.

"Dave, I'm getting a glare off that water. Can you
bring me in close there, or better yet, back off for a
long shot?"

The electronic image blurred as the camera swung
its eye away from the water hazard. The scope widened
on the screen, encompassing a fairway lined with a

large, colorfully dressed crowd. In the distance, on the TV's horizon, a quartet of players were moving after their previous shots, each to a different part of the fairway.

"Close in on the guy in the green shirt," the director said.

"But he's way in the back," the cameramen told him.

"I know," the director said. "Let's have a closeup anyway. This guy made quite a charge in New York a few months ago. I think maybe he has a future."

The image being broadcast over the airwaves was part of the action on the far side of the course, but the director kept one eye on Thurmond Leaner's monitor as Leaner walked toward his next shot. There was a determination in his step that the director noted, an air of confidence. And a sort of windmill motion that Leaner made with his right arm preceding his shot. The director was crazy about golf and he loved a fellow who gave some drama to the game. Too many of the players tended to be blond, blue-eyed, lean—clones of each other. Too few ex-caddies and hustlers like Trevino and Ballesteros, too many sun-belt guys coddled by sponsors and scholarships. And Leaner photographed well, too. He didn't merit special attention just by some antics or gestures. The director couldn't nail it down, but Leaner somehow filled the screen whenever he was on...with his body language, his expression or, like a moment ago, with an unexpected movement. He ran an instant replay of Leaner's clockwise motion of his arm before settling down for the shot. It was almost like a pitcher's windup. A caption summed up the image for the Saturday afternoon TV audience. "LEANER

+ 2," it said. Over the television sets the commentators praised Leaner's performance.

"A beautiful approach shot to the fifteenth green there by Leaner a moment ago. He's a little off the pace but still within striking distance of the lead. He's also a modest young man. Speaking to us yesterday, he said, 'I've still got a lot to learn. About a lot of things, golf included.' A welcome addition to the tour. Now back to Chris on Seventeen...."

For viewers at home Leaner was little more than a temporary blip on the screen while they put away a bottle of beer, but even minor fame was more than Leaner ever expected. Besides, fame wasn't what he was after. It didn't do a thing for your head, except maybe turn it.

As he walked along the fairway he reached out for the jug of water his caddy was handing him. Autumn had arrived, but the sweat poured off his face. He looked over to the gallery, taking a long pull on the water.

"I lost sight of her," Leaner said to the caddy. "Where did she go?"

"She moved over by that sycamore there."

"Oh, yes..."

Lauren had elbowed her way to the ropes, and Leaner now went up to her while the others were taking their next shots.

"I'm glad you came with me," he said. "It means a lot to me."

"Well, we're in this together." She smiled happily.

Leaner squeezed her hand and walked onto the green. The weather was stifling, his cotton shirt soaked through. He crouched down close to the green, study-

ing the break and the grain, aiming the putter as if he
were laying out a set of floor plans, looking for the best
possible line to take. Bearing down on him from above
was another TV platform. The media coverage bothered
him not at all. He touched off the putt, and it dropped
solidly in the center of the cup, the birdie edging him
closer to par for the tournament. Some applause broke
out, and Leaner waved the ball in the air to show his
appreciation.

He massaged his arm on the walk to the next tee.
He was still sometimes apprehensive that it might have
healed improperly, remembering how, when the doc-
tors removed the cast, he had worried that they would
find a shriveled-up little noodle of a limb. He was experiencing a touch of soreness now, but it seemed to
be muscular. The early anxiety about his arm had disappeared the moment he lifted a club again. He had
hit a bucket of balls, packed the car, and was off once
more. Some answers eluded him, but he *knew* that this
was now his life. Using the airlines would be more
practical, but Leaner preferred doing it his own way.
Besides, he could be spelled in the driving now that he
had company on the road. Working as a team also kept
him out of trouble. Look at the entourage race car drivers had. For sure, no way could they do it without a
pit crew....

Leaner now drove his ball down the fairway. Its tra-
jectory was like a jet taking off, a low path that hugged
the ground, biting the air in a steep climb, then bouncing an additional sixty yards after landing. He had placed
the ball in a near-perfect position for his approach shot
to the green. He handed the club over to the caddy and
moved up the fairway. He felt at ease, and suspected

that it had something to do with professionalism. The PGA circuit was the real thing, not the malarky he ran into his first time out of the chute.

He took the iron he'd decided on and made a shot that was less than he'd hoped for. It had called for a solid six iron and he had tried a let-up five to make sure he made the green. The ball hadn't pulled up in time. He'd overclubbed.

"Forget it," the caddy told him.

"Thanks," Leaner said, meaning it. "Have you seen...? Never mind, I see her over there."

Leaner once again made a detour to the fringes of the gallery.

"Have I told you lately how really crazy I am about you?" he asked her.

"Yes." She smiled as only she could. "Just this morning."

"Would you do something for me?"

"Have I ever denied my man anything?"

"Just wet your lips a little. Maybe open your mouth slightly."

Running her tongue across her lips, Margot Catalina grinned and showed her teeth, fluffing up her hair as a bonus, allowing some of it to fall across her face.

"Wow," Leaner said.

He returned to the middle of the fairway and surveyed the landscape. As he walked, his caddy fell in at his side. "Can I ask you something?" he said.

"Shoot."

"I've been watching you for three days now and, well, if it's none of my business just say so. But do these two ladies know each other, or do you have to keep them apart? I mean, what's going on? What's the deal?"

Leaner wondered how to answer him. A summary of the situation would tell nothing but some facts...I knew Lauren first, then I met Margot, and then I ended up in the hospital with my sister at my bedside and Lauren my wife and Margot my girl getting chummy in the corridor.... That would sound kinkier than it was. Unquestionably there were some new logistics to hammer out when Margot moved back to Texas with him and Lauren. The unusual thing about it all, in Leaner's eyes, was that none of it had been his idea. The two women had worked it all out between them while he lay in the hospital, dead to the world. To date, their worst household flare-up had been over who wasn't refilling the ice tray after emptying it. (It was Leaner.) And the ice business apparently wasn't a domestic red herring, an escape valve for a deeper problem. They had agreed to work things out by majority rule, and they genuinely enjoyed each other's company too much to gang up on any one member of the crew. Lauren and Margot were no more part of Leaner's harem than he was of theirs. True, the women did tend to pamper him while he was in a tournament, but that only made sense for all of them.

The only thing Leaner knew for sure was that no one was perfect, certainly not him, nor either of the women with whom he shared his life. At the least they blunted each other's hard edges of self-centeredness, and more often than not they had a way of bringing out the best in each other, something none of them had ever been able to do alone. Their house spilled over with laughter. Each shared themselves with the other two, and there seemed more than enough to go around.

Leaner stood alongside the caddy while one of his

foursome took his shot. He wasn't sure he had a complete answer to the caddy's question ... anyway, not one that he could manage under these circumstances.

What he said was, "We sort of take care of each other."

And, so far as it went, that was the magical truth of it.